THE
DIVORCE

BOOKS BY VICTORIA JENKINS

The Girls in the Water
The First one to Die
Nobody's Child
A Promise to the Dead

THE
DIVORCE

VICTORIA JENKINS

Bookouture

Published by Bookouture in 2019

An imprint of StoryFire Ltd.

Carmelite House
50 Victoria Embankment
London EC4Y 0DZ

www.bookouture.com

ISBN: 978-1-78681-941-3
eBook ISBN: 978-1-78681-985-7

ONE

KAREN

I meet them for the first time on a wet and dreary Thursday morning, a relentless downpour pelting the ground so loudly it almost drowns out the sound of my introduction. They are barely visible beneath the black umbrella he holds above them, her head dipped towards his chest to protect her from an onslaught of driving rain that has been tirelessly battering the street since the early hours. It seems ironic that in this moment, to anyone looking on from the street, this couple might appear so close, so together. Yet they wouldn't be here if that were the case.

'I'm Karen,' I say, ushering them into the hallway, extending a hand first to Lydia Green and then to her husband, Josh. 'Lovely to meet you both.'

Lydia's hand is cold to the touch, her slim fingers icy against mine. She offers me a small smile as she steps aside and shrugs her rain-sodden jacket from her slender shoulders. She thanks me as I take it from her, and I recognise the east London accent that I detected during our phone conversation, its tones muted and restrained; the kind of lilt that suggests a person has made a conscious effort to lose any trace of their roots from their voice.

When Josh reaches for my hand, his fingers linger on mine a moment too long. The men are usually more nervous than the women when they first arrive here, more anxious about what lies ahead, as though accepting their marriage needs help is an admission of failure on their part. For many, this anxiety manifests itself in handshakes that are too tight, ill-timed comments intended to fill uncomfortable lulls in conversation; sometimes just the silences, left to fester until someone finds a distraction.

'What a beautiful house,' Lydia says, casting her eyes up the staircase. I notice them flit along the montage of framed photographs that climbs the wall: an array of travel snaps taken on holidays over the years. Another row lines the hallway wall, and I wait as her attention runs along each in turn, absorbing the snapshot moments of my past.

'Thank you. It was a shell when we moved in. It took years to renovate.'

As I watch her scan the place admiringly, I remember the surge of pride I used to feel swelling in my chest whenever someone came into my home and made a comment such as this. Decades ago, I walked along this street as a teenage girl, never once imagining that years later I might live here. I would have pinched myself had someone told me that this was where my future would lie, not believing that such a fate could await someone with my humble background. Yet nothing here looks as it once did. These material things for which Sean and I worked so hard seem insignificant now, yet I know I continue to cling to their sheen in the hope that they'll detract from the reality that sits just behind them, waiting to rear its head and knock me sideways when I least expect it.

'Can I hang that up for you?' I reach past Lydia to take Josh's jacket from him. He has stepped back and stands just behind his wife, his wet coat still on, moving from foot to foot as though warming himself up: from the cold outside or for what's about to come, I can't yet tell. He is tall, but looks younger than his wife – he would pass for late twenties though I know he is much older – with a boyish youthfulness in the flush of his skin and his dark hair styled in a way that might be regarded as fashionable, short at the sides and long on top. He is dressed smartly, in pressed chinos and a white shirt that looks so crisp he might be wearing it for the first time.

Beside him, Lydia is wearing a floral tea dress and a mauve cardigan, and her dark brown hair is pinned back into a bun. There is something demure and almost dated about her appearance. I wouldn't have picked them out of a busy room as a couple, but this is nothing out of the ordinary: the most unlikely of couples are often the ones who survive the day-to-day challenges of married life, even when it might seem that the obstacles they face are too great for them to overcome. I wonder what this couple's problems are, having requested my help in doing just that.

Josh passes me his coat, thanking me with a smile. It is different to the one offered by his wife, more strained and less sincere; it is given and retracted so quickly that he seems almost resentful at being made to part with it. I wonder whether he is happy to be here. Occasionally, only one half of a couple really wants to attend these sessions, despite what the other might claim or hope for. In those cases, my job becomes almost impossible. I have an eighty per cent success rate, which I take a lot of pride in. I have received thank-you presents from clients after blocks of sessions have come to an end: flowers, wine, handwritten letters thanking me for saving a relationship; in many cases, for keeping a family together. I save a token gesture from each gift – a card, a dried petal, a label removed from a bottle – and store them all in a box, and on days when I feel my life no longer serves a purpose, I return to it. It reminds me that I am still needed by someone.

'Follow me through.'

I lead them down the hallway to the back of the house, bypassing the door to the kitchen and taking them through to my consultancy room. I have worked from home for almost two decades now; before that, I was in Islington, in a soulless office block in which troubled couples would pour out their problems to me while overlooking the web of traffic that crept through the streets below. I am happier seeing clients at the house, and I believe they are more relaxed here. I can offer them a more comfortable setting, and decent coffee that doesn't taste like day-old dishwater.

'Can I get either of you a drink before we start?' I ask, pushing the door to the consultancy room open and ushering them through. Lydia enters first, taking a moment to assess her surroundings: the cream sofa that lines the far wall, the patterned chair in the corner, the sideboard, the bookcase stocked with an array of the literature I have accumulated over the years, the view through the window over the long rectangle of back garden. I have done what I can to keep this room as homely and comfortable as possible, in keeping with the rest of the house. I want my clients to feel at ease here. I want them to feel that within these four walls they can say the things they may feel unable to articulate elsewhere.

Josh follows us into the room.

'Tea? Coffee?'

'Not for me, thanks,' he says.

'Tea would be lovely,' Lydia says, turning to me. 'Just milk, please.'

'I'll be a couple of minutes. Make yourselves comfortable.'

I leave them in the room together and pull the door to behind me, making sure to leave it only slightly ajar. They will be able to hear me in the kitchen making tea if they choose to listen out for it: the clicking of the kettle's switch; the soft thud of a closed cupboard door. Similarly, I will be able to hear them before they see me return with the drinks. Though it's a slightly underhand method – something I'm sure would be considered unorthodox by some – it's one I have employed for years now. It has enabled me to steal snippets of conversation that have in some cases offered me more insight than hours' worth of sessions, and at times my eavesdropping has proved invaluable. It has allowed me to see who is here because they want to be and who has been brought here under duress, having finally yielded to the demands of what they perceive as a nagging partner.

What I know of this couple is for now limited to the details I gained from Lydia in one of her emails. I know that she is thirty-four, her husband forty-one. I know that they have been together for fourteen years and have two children, a girl aged thirteen and a boy aged nine. These few facts are enough to throw up a range of questions, ones I'm sure I'll begin to find answers to once the two of them start to talk.

Wondering just how quickly into their relationship Lydia became pregnant, I make a pot of tea and take three cups from the cupboard, just in case Josh changes his mind. I fill a small jug with milk and add sugar to the bowl. The tea set was a wedding present from one of Sean's aunts, and until a few months ago it hadn't been taken from its box in years. I had always saved it for 'best', whenever that might have proved to be. There is a saying about saving things for special occasions, about life itself being the special occasion, and I have lost enough now to understand just what that means.

While I make the tea, I contemplate the same things that cross my mind during every introductory session I hold with my clients. What are my first impressions of them, individually and as a couple? Do I believe at this moment that I will be able to help them? Sometimes, just a few minutes are enough to know whether counselling will benefit a couple or not. When someone makes it clear they don't want to be here – which happens surprisingly regularly – there is often no point in holding even the first session. There have been times when I have said as much. For any marriage to survive, both partners need to be fully invested in making the relationship work.

I am unsure of what to make of Josh. I saw the way he looked at me when I answered the door to them, the way his eyes silently scanned his surroundings before moving quickly on, passing over the house before resting on me briefly, staring at and through me then looking away, dismissing me as soon as he had acknowledged my presence. I saw the way he looked at his wife when I left the room to come to the kitchen, resentment all too evident in his steely, distant eyes.

As I leave the kitchen with the tea tray in my hands, my attention is caught by the hallway wall and the line of photographs that runs along it. I stop, unsure for a moment whether my eyes are playing tricks on me. When I step closer, I realise I have made no mistake. Each of the photographs – eight of them in total – is hanging off centre, knocked at an angle that makes it lean to the left. As though someone has run a hand along the wall, hitting each frame in turn.

I am sure that when Josh and Lydia arrived, the photographs were straight. I am meticulous in the details of this house to the point at which I appreciate it may be considered by some obsessive behaviour, but spending so much of my time within these walls makes this place both my office and my home. If any of the photographs hadn't been straight, I would have noticed earlier, and didn't I not long ago watch Lydia study them admiringly? I would have noticed then if they were all at an angle.

The tea tray is heavy in my hands, its weight putting pressure on my left wrist. I adjust the balance of it and head to the consultancy room, shaking myself from the suspicious, uneasy thoughts that are attempting to take root in my brain. I must have simply not noticed that the photographs needed straightening. If not, then either Lydia or Josh must have brushed past them as they walked down the hallway. It is easily done, after all.

I wait a couple of feet outside the door of the consultancy room, listening for the sound of their voices. There is a rustle of cushions as one of them shifts on the sofa; a moment later, Josh exhales noisily.

'This is madness.'

'Please,' Lydia says. 'Not now.'

'We shouldn't be here.' His words are taut, their endings clipped.

Lydia says nothing for a moment, but I hear another rustling noise, this time as though she is searching through her bag. I wait for Josh to say something more – to offer some further protestation at being brought here under apparent duress – but there is nothing. A moment later, I push open the door and place the tea tray on the coffee table that sits between the sofa and the chair. It is usual for my clients to sit on the sofa, whether next to each other or at opposite ends, but Lydia has taken my chair in the corner and Josh is standing at the window, his back turned to the room and to his wife.

I appear to startle her as I enter the room; she drops her bag on the floor and gives me a nervous smile. She looks at her husband's back and offers me a glance that seems to act as an apology, as though she already feels the need to excuse his apparent lack of interest.

'There's a spare cup for you here, Josh, if you change your mind.'

'Thanks.' He sits on the sofa and I move to the other end, positioned now between them. I think for a moment about asking Lydia to swap with me, but there is an obvious atmosphere already making the room feel uncomfortable, and the sooner it is erased, the better for us all. I don't want to embarrass her any more than her husband already appears to be doing.

'Okay,' I say, smoothing the front of my skirt as I settle in my seat. 'As I said when we spoke on the phone, this first session gives me an opportunity to learn about you and your relationship and gives you both a chance to be honest about what makes you happy in the relationship and what you'd like to see change. I'd like each of you in your own time to tell me the story of you, as you see it – how you met and what you liked about the other person in those early days. Tell me the things you're unhappy with now, the things that you'd like to see made different if you could. Which of you would like to start us off?'

Lydia looks to her husband, but Josh is staring at the carpet between his feet. There is something about him that I just can't isolate; not yet, anyway, though I'm confident it will come to me in time. He has been polite enough, thanking me when it has been necessary, but it has evidently been forced and taken an effort.

'Lydia,' I say. 'How about you go first? Where did you two meet?'

Lydia glances at Josh again, as though seeking his approval to answer the question. He meets her eye briefly, then looks away, averting his attention to the window and the stretch of garden that lies beyond. Despite the grey gloom and the rain that continues to pummel the lawn relentlessly, it is obvious where much of my time is spent these days when I'm not working. Gardening has turned out to be a kind of therapy; one of the few things that allows me to switch off from my life – from what is left of it – for an hour or two.

'Through a mutual friend,' she says, looking back at me. 'Someone we both used to work with.'

'What is it you do, Lydia?'

'I'm an administrator. Of sorts. Was, rather. I mean, it's all very boring. I quit work when I had the kids.'

It occurs to me that whatever type of administration it was, Lydia couldn't have worked for very long. She would have been twenty-one when she gave birth to her daughter, so her career would have been short. I notice her use of the adverb 'I'. *When I had the kids*, rather than *when we had the kids*. Perhaps I'm looking too deeply into things. It was a habit that used to irritate Sean about me, particularly during a disagreement. *You analyse every word*, he would say, before quickly rephrasing whatever vocabulary I had jumped upon, as though in the hope that by changing the words he could change the intention. In my experience, people admit far more unwittingly than they ever might intentionally. Often, single words can say far more than whole sentences.

I wonder about the children and how they might perceive their parents' relationship, but I decide not to pursue that aspect of the marriage just yet. There will be plenty of time to discuss them during later sessions, and for now my priority is trying to find out as much as I can about these people – as individuals and as a couple. Not wanting to overload them with too many questions for the time being, I return the focus to how they met, giving Lydia a nod of encouragement to continue her version of events, as that is all anyone is able to give: a version. People rarely recount an event as it actually happened, and no two people will ever give the same version, making the truth of anything hard to come by.

'You were telling me how you met,' I prompt her.

'It was at a party – this mutual friend I mentioned, it was her birthday. We got chatting at the bar.'

She stops and looks at her hands in her lap, idly twisting her engagement ring between the thumb and forefinger of her right hand. It is an eye-catching piece of jewellery with a large stone that catches the light. I think of my own engagement ring, so lovingly selected and yet perhaps so unfashionable by today's standards. I can recall the moment Sean proposed to me as though it was just this morning; as though the two and a half decades that have passed since that day have been imagined in the space between breakfast and now. I can still taste the pizza we shared, the lager he drank – lager that I stole in sips from his glass, regretting my attempts at sophistication by opting for the house red – the smell of the aftershave he wore and that lingered on my own clothing for the rest of that weekend in Florence. And that look on his face when he drew the ring box from his jacket pocket, placing it casually on the table between us before mimicking my look of surprise – I can picture it now as though he is still sitting opposite me.

Whatever problems you think you have, I want to say to Josh and Lydia, *just let them go. You are young and you're together and you're alive. Make the most of everything while everything is what you have.*

But of course, I can't say these things. I can't tell them that sometimes life is just hard and that the same applies to everyone, regardless of status or age or wealth. That would be far too honest, and it is something that no one wants to hear. Most people want the reassurance of a solution, even in situations where the possibility of one might not exist.

I look again at the ring. It is large and showy; it seems an unlikely choice for a woman who appears as reserved as Lydia, though it might be possible that it was presented to her as a surprise, in much the same way mine was. Maybe it reflects how Josh regards her, which may be very different to the way Lydia sees herself. I wonder if it once suited her, and whether the woman Josh proposed to was a different person to the woman who is sitting opposite him today.

I look at her and widen my eyes, encouraging her once again to continue. 'You were at the bar,' I remind her, though it is my own mind that has wandered for a moment. 'What did you talk about?'

'I don't remember the details,' she admits. 'Well, if I'm honest, I wasn't really looking for anything, not at that time, anyway. We talked a bit, about the party mostly, I think, and when I went home, I didn't really expect to see him again.'

'Why not?'

'She probably couldn't remember any of it.' Josh speaks to the window, as though thinking aloud, his statement not really directed at either of us. The words are scathing and dismissive and I see the reaction they burn into Lydia's face. She doesn't meet my eye, too embarrassed by her husband's shaming of her in front of someone who is still for now little more than a stranger.

'I'd had a couple of drinks,' she says, as though she feels the need to explain or defend herself.

'A couple of bottles.'

She looks at me, her eyes pleading with mine as though willing me to ask her husband to stop what he is doing. Her face is flushed slightly, drawing colour into her pale cheeks. She might be an attractive woman, but a tiredness pulls at her features and there are dark shadows beneath her eyes. I say nothing in response to Josh's comment, though it obviously raises questions. I don't want to give attention to behaviour that is unkind, so instead I move the focus back to Lydia. He will get a chance to give his version of their meeting. I wonder which of their accounts will be closest to the truth. Sometimes it's easier to lie to yourself than it is to accept a truth that was always there but was never wanted.

'You say you didn't expect to see Josh again. Why was that?'

'I don't know. You know how it is,' she says, as though we've known each other for years, just two friends meeting up for a coffee and a chat. 'Men like Josh and women like me …'

She trails into silence and looks down at her hands again, and I think I see one of the problems here. Looking at Josh, my suspicions are perhaps confirmed. He eyes his wife with a sideways glare, his gaze concentrated on her face and his frustrations with her almost tangible in the air between the three of us. Lydia flattens her hair against the side of her head before picking at a thumbnail, in what appears to be a concentrated effort not to make eye contact with either Josh or me. Her anxiety is palpable, infusing the air around us. Is she always this self-deprecating? I wonder. Does he always respond to her self-criticism with such obvious impatience?

'Women like you,' I repeat. 'What do you mean by that?'

I already know exactly what she is suggesting, but to get to the root of this relationship's problems I need to hear her truths as Lydia sees them. There is evidently a confidence issue here, and I wonder whether it is historically embedded within her, or whether Josh has in some way contributed to her lack of self-belief.

Josh has so far shown little more than hostility, but I realise it would be unfair of me to judge him on this first assessment alone. His response is natural, perhaps, in the way that so many people react to these initial sessions with reluctance and apathy, not quite sure of themselves, or in some cases, too sure. I remind myself that until I know and see more of him and his relationship with his wife, I must remain neutral. Living with someone who is constantly negative, someone who berates themselves for everything in the way it already appears Lydia might do, may be as challenging as living with someone who believes they can do no wrong. And things are often very different behind closed doors.

'I don't know,' she replies, repeating the phrase that acts as a prefix to much of what she says. 'I just didn't expect him to notice me.' She presses her hair behind her ears, though none has fallen loose from where it is carefully pinned in place. 'Men like Josh don't look twice at women like me.'

Josh emits a noise, a snort that seems to make light of his wife's feelings, and it does nothing to help the awkwardness that has fallen over the room.

'And yet he obviously made the effort to contact you again after that first meeting,' I say, suspecting there is little chance it was Lydia who pursued the relationship. She doesn't seem to me the type of woman who would ask a man if he wanted to go for a drink, not if her response to his initial attention is anything to judge her character by.

'Exactly,' Josh adds, in a tone that is at once exasperated and edged with a smug gratitude.

Lydia nods. 'I was at work a few days later and suddenly there he was,' she says, smiling at the memory. 'He said he was just passing, but I knew that was a lie – he didn't work or live anywhere near the place. He asked me out for a drink after work and I couldn't find an excuse not to go.'

'Charming,' Josh says, and when he speaks this time it is accompanied by the faintest hint of a smile. He is better-looking when he smiles, I notice: the harder edges of his face soften, and his eyes seem to warm from their grey coolness. His nose is crooked at the bridge; it appears to have been broken at some point. I wonder what happened to him: whether the injury was accidental or the result of something more.

'You know what I mean.'

In this moment – as in that moment at the front door earlier – no one would believe that this couple has any problems, or at the very least no problems that merit seeking the help of a marriage guidance counsellor. I wonder how their relationship looks to those outside their home yet still close enough to care about them – parents, siblings, friends. Couples in crisis often act out the marriage they wish they had when in the company of others, with many doing an effective job at convincing those who love them that everything is fine even when it isn't. But performances like that are hard to maintain long-term. Eventually the truth escapes through the cracks and the reality of the situation warps the veneer that has been so carefully constructed.

I am always a last resort. By the time they come to me for help, most couples have already discussed the very real possibility of divorce.

'And what then?' I ask.

Lydia licks her lips nervously, knowing she is expected to say far more than she has so far offered. I lean forward and pour her a cup of tea; she adds milk and sips it carefully, all the while avoiding her husband's eyes. From where I am sitting, I watch them both, conscious not to make it too obvious that I am doing so. She is anxious and on edge, constantly fiddling with something: the hair that is pinned back so precisely, the rings that adorn her slender fingers, the deep blue hemline of her dress. He, meanwhile, continues to radiate a hostility that can be felt like the heat of a flame, his angular jaw set in defiance and his face stamped with a permanent expression of irritability.

'We arranged a time and a place, and I popped home after work to get changed before meeting him at the pub. It was nice, you know ...' She trails off as embarrassment creeps up into her cheeks in a mottle of pink that sits upon the flush already settled there. 'I'm sorry. I've never done anything like this before. It's a bit weird talking about it all like this, especially to a stranger. Sorry, I don't mean any offence by that. I don't really know what to say.'

'It's okay,' I reassure her. 'Take your time. If it's easier, try to imagine I'm not here. Don't tell me about it – tell Josh.'

Lydia shifts in the chair and takes a breath as though she is about to embark upon a recital. I take this moment to study her: her hands in her lap, her fingers restless; her shoulders hunched, her body bracing itself. Though she is in her thirties, there is something older about the conservative way she dresses. There is a nervousness about her that makes itself known in every movement and gesture, that makes everything around her seem unstable in some way, as though her own uncertainty is left like a trail of crumbs behind her wherever she moves, visible to anyone who might care enough to look. She is hesitant when she speaks, seeming to assess every word before she allows it to leave her mouth, and I wonder whose benefit her caution is for.

'I made the mistake of saying I hadn't eaten anything since breakfast, and you insisted on getting us dinner, do you remember? I wouldn't order anything, so you chose what you wanted and then ordered the same for me. Lamb, I think it was. It wasn't particularly nice, but I ate it so as not to offend you.' She turns to me. 'I hate eating in front of people. I'd never normally have dinner on a first date – I don't think most people do, do they? There's always that worry about spilling something on yourself or getting something stuck in your teeth, and if anyone's going to do something daft, it's always likely to be me.'

She laughs nervously, seeming embarrassed at the speed at which her words have fallen from her. Looking down at her hands in her lap, she lapses into silence, as though immediately regretting having said so much. There is something vulnerable about this woman. Her anxiety makes the room feel small and constricting.

'That's not how it happened,' Josh says, shaking his head but directing his comment at me. 'She couldn't make a decision, so she asked me to choose something for her.'

There's something defensive in his tone, as though he feels himself under attack by Lydia. The way he addresses me when it was his wife who spoke to him implies a dismissiveness that is already beginning to appear to be second nature to him.

A silence follows.

'Did I?'

Josh tuts as though dealing with an argumentative child, and I wonder if he always treats her in this way. This short amount of time has already allowed me an insight into his personality, and what he has shown of himself so far does little to endear him to an onlooker. I know how it feels to live with someone who trivialises your feelings and belittles you as though for fun. I know the effects of being spoken down to and made to feel like less than nothing, how over time these things chip the edges off you and change your shape, altering your very form. I wonder if the Lydia who sits beside me today is different to the one who existed before Josh, and if so, just how altered she is.

Josh sighs heavily and shifts on the sofa. It is obvious already that he is not engaged in the session, and it is starting to feel as though his very being here is an inconvenience to him. 'You know, I found it charming at first,' he says, 'the way she deliberated over everything. It was flattering to be relied upon to make choices; it felt like I was earning her trust. Gets a bit wearing after a while, though.' He sits back and folds his arms across his chest, a defensive action that creates a divide between him and Lydia. Between him and me. 'She's just not very good at making decisions. She never seems to know what she wants.'

She. That single word used yet again says so much more than it might at first suggest. I am trying not to make a snap judgement of Josh, but he isn't making it easy for me to see anything through the hostility radiating from him.

'How did you feel after that first evening you spent together?'

Lydia picks at the nail of her left thumb again. 'Good. I mean … it was nice, obviously.' She looks at her husband and smiles, though the gesture is not reciprocated. 'We swapped numbers and said we'd do it again sometime. And that sometime turned out to be the following weekend, I think. We went to the theatre – there was a show on that I must have mentioned. He went and bought tickets, as a surprise.'

Romantic, I think. The act appears in complete contradiction to everything that Josh has managed to present of himself during the short time they've been here. It is an indicator that he listened to Lydia during that first date; really listened, and not just in the way that people often seem to, mostly thinking about what they want to say next. I have seen so many of those people in this room, men and women: people who talk but don't hear; people who speak relentlessly but say very little.

What happened between that first date and now that so dramatically changed the way he behaves towards her?

Perhaps my initial judgement of Josh is unfair – and it is true that despite the necessity to appear neutral, impartiality is almost impossible, and judgement is inevitable. Maybe I have got him wrong: perhaps he is one of those rare listeners, someone who says little but takes everything in, preferring to maintain a silence until he has something meaningful to offer to a conversation. His few words today may simply be evidence of this, and yet I can't place a finger on the reason why I already doubt it.

'What was it called?'

'Sorry?' Lydia looks at Josh, a flicker of panic flitting across her face, and I wonder why she seems so flustered by the question.

'The show,' he says flatly. 'What was it called?'

Lydia looks at me and smiles. 'I can't remember now,' she says, waving a hand as though to shoo away her forgetfulness. 'I've got a shocking memory, really I have. I need to write things down otherwise they go out of my head again within seconds. I remember I enjoyed it, though.'

Ignoring her, Josh turns to direct his response to me. 'It was called *The Playing Field*. It was a local production about a group of graduates: where their lives took them after university and how fate brought them all back together. She loved it, but it was awful. Like watching a bunch of sixth-form students fail a drama exam.'

He adopts a different voice for this last statement, making his tone deeper as though to mimic someone. He holds my gaze for a moment longer than is comfortable, and I look away. The weight of his stare reminds me of someone else, taking me back to a time I have tried for years to put to the back of my mind, though I know that no matter what I do, those days will never be forgotten. He is out of my life, but he will never be truly gone.

'But you stayed for the duration, for Lydia's sake,' I say, speaking to Josh but directing the words at his wife. 'To give her something you knew would make her happy,' I add, confirming it as fact rather than offering it as a question.

Josh shrugs. 'Of course. That's what you do, isn't it?'

Not everyone does, I think. Some people only see their own wants, their own needs.

'I remember now,' Lydia says. 'Of course I do.' She smiles, first at her husband and then at me. 'I'd really wanted to see it, but I had no one else to go with.'

'Are you sure you remember?' Josh says, his tone unnecessarily challenging. 'I mean, this is one of the problems, isn't it?' he continues, throwing the words at her. 'Your memory isn't that reliable. How much do you actually remember of anything? She only seems to recall the bad bits,' he says, turning to me. 'It's like everything that was ever good has just been wiped from her memory.'

This is the most Josh has said, and it tells me something more about their relationship and why they are here, the shades of grey that pattern the two of them together beginning to form a picture as they speak. They were happy, once. For whatever reason, it seems their versions of the past are very different, though this is not uncommon between two people who have experienced so much together yet are shaped by life differently enough to view their shared history in contrast. It is true that while the human brain can easily forget names, places and events, it is usually able to remember feelings. We may not recall exactly what happened, but we are able to remember how something made us feel.

'It's quite usual for that to happen,' I tell him. 'Sometimes our brains focus on the negative and we appear to forget the good. It doesn't mean the happy memories aren't there – there are ways we can bring them back. It's actually a lot more common than people realise.'

It can work the other way as well. People forget the bad and focus only on the good, as though blocking out anything that might stain the image of a time or a person they have imprinted upon their mind. It often happens this way following a death. Once someone is gone, only the goodness in their character remains in the memory of the person who loved them, as though they personified perfection, elevated to a saintly status once there is nothing tangible to contradict the illusion. No one is without flaws, though these flaws become lost to the memory once memory is all that remains.

Perhaps I am guilty of doing the same where Sean is concerned, although in his case there were so few flaws to be found. He was patient when I most needed him to be; he was understanding of things that I was unable to put into words or explain even to myself. We met at a time when I believed myself incapable of love – of loving another person or of being loved by someone else – and he managed to restore most of what my first husband had taken from me and broken. Sean was one of those rare beings, an anomaly among humans: an almost-perfect.

'That's not true,' Lydia says, objecting to her husband's accusation. 'It's just it sometimes feels as though the bad has started to outweigh the good, that's all.'

I watch her as she speaks; she is staring at Josh with an expression that doesn't change, her eyes glassy, seeming to gaze beyond his. Her face is difficult to read at times – as difficult as his is – but I find these types of clients the most fascinating, relishing the challenge that getting to know them in more colour offers me.

'What makes you feel this way, Lydia?' I ask. 'When you say "bad", what are you referring to?'

Her eyes leave Josh's face and she casts her focus to her lap for a moment before finally looking at me. 'I don't know,' she says with a shrug. 'Just life, I suppose.' She laughs, the sound forced. 'If living was easy, everyone would be doing it, wouldn't they?'

There is no humour in the words or in the tone with which they are delivered; instead, her gaze rests on me as though she is silently trying to communicate something else. When I look at Josh, his expression tells me that he too realises his wife longs to tell me more than she feels able to. He is glaring at her, his cool grey eyes fixed in a hard stare.

'I'd say your life is pretty good, all things considered,' he tells her coldly.

Lydia sits back and offers me a small smile as she adjusts herself in her seat. Her hair is pulled too tightly against her head, making it look as though it must be giving her a headache. There is something prim and harsh about her appearance, as though she is trying to make herself less attractive than I suspect she really is. I wonder what she looked like on their wedding day; if, all those years ago, she was unrecognisable from the woman who sits here today. Does Josh regard himself as living with a different person to the one he exchanged vows with; can the same be said for Lydia too? Too often people come to believe themselves deceived. They expected one thing; they ended up with something else entirely.

My first husband, Damien, reminded me regularly that I wasn't the girl he had married. 'I didn't sign up for this,' he would say, as though my silences and dark moods had been disguised during the early days of our relationship in an attempt to trap him. When stress made me lose weight, he would tell me I was getting too thin. When I ate, I was greedy and getting too fat. If I stayed at home, I was lazy; if I went out, I would be accused of being with other men. It was no wonder I was no longer the girl he had married, though he could never see that he was responsible for what I had become.

'Lydia,' I say, wrenching my mind from thoughts of Damien Hunter. 'Tell me what you liked about Josh when you first met.'

We wait a few moments as she composes her answer. Is she being careful not to offend or upset him, I wonder, or is she genuinely struggling to remember the things that had attracted her to her husband all those years ago?

'He was nice,' she says eventually. 'I mean, I know that sounds a bit boring, but isn't nice what most people want really, even if they don't realise it at the time?' She dips her head and runs a hand over her hair, taking her eyes from me for a moment. 'He was kind. He was attentive.' She looks at Josh, who has been listening intently to her every word. 'He was a good man.'

I note her use of the past tense. *He was a good man.* So what is he now?

'How have things changed for you, Lydia? Josh, you'll have a chance to give your thoughts on all this in a moment.'

I offer him a smile, but nothing is returned. He is too preoccupied with studying his wife, his focus fixed on her face as though trying to bore into her brain to see what lies within. He is looking at her as though he is unsure who she is. It's an expression I have seen on the faces of so many people who have sat with me in this room, as if entering the place has made their partner someone different, someone they fail to recognise once they're removed from the familiarity of their everyday surroundings. Being here seems to offer an opportunity to say the things that can't be aired anywhere else, and sometimes this is all that is needed for old wounds to be finally healed without leaving scars.

In other cases, it has been the very thing that has dragged a marriage to its painful and messy end.

'I just …' Lydia waits, seeming to be gauging Josh's possible reaction to whatever it is she is about to say. 'It's probably just a marriage thing, isn't it? I mean, so many years down the line, it's never going to be the same as it was when you first met.' She fiddles with the hem of her dress, smoothing it out between her thumb and forefinger. She is right, of course, but there is obviously far more going on here than the simple loss of a honeymoon period.

'When we spoke on the phone, you mentioned frequent arguments. Can you tell me what they tend to be about?'

Lydia takes a deep breath and exhales loudly, hissing out air between pursed lips. She pushes her fingertips to her right eye, and I notice for the first time how long her make-up-free lashes are. She isn't a conventionally pretty woman, not what many would consider to be beautiful, but there is something attractive about her; something sharp and angular that exudes a certain kind of sexy. It is contradictory to everything that is evident in her character.

'We just don't seem to get along any more, not like we used to. He works a lot and when he's home we just … I don't know. The bickering seems endless. He's tired a lot of the time—'

'Because of work.'

Lydia sucks in her top lip. 'I get that, but sometimes you make me feel … I don't know. Like I'm not important enough to you.'

Josh rolls his eyes. 'You've had everything,' he says defensively. 'You live in a lovely house, you wear nice clothes, you go on expensive holidays.' He looks at me and shrugs, his hands flung skywards as though admitting defeat; as though all these references to material stability should be enough to justify anything else that might lie beneath the surface. 'What more does she want?'

I think of the number of couples who have had this same conversation in this same room. I could spend the rest of the day contemplating the mistake so many people make in considering material possessions their priority. The most intelligent, well-balanced people get drawn into this same trap: this race to make money and to have, have, have, as though consumption is the key to success and ownership is the measure of a happy life. I feel justified in saying it because I have been one of these people, at a time when I believed that wealth equated power and belongings would buy me a status that would somehow keep me protected. And then I found out that that isn't the case, and with this realisation came the crushing truth that all of it is meaningless and that time is the thing that makes you powerful, while you still have enough of it.

I should have known it already, years earlier, but the impression of a successful life was used as a shroud to cover everything I had experienced in my first marriage, as though hiding what had happened behind a glossy veneer could take away the truth of its existence. I wanted to earn money; I wanted to have nice things. My home would present a reality that couldn't be further from the one I'd left behind in my old life: a life in which I had next to nothing, and what little I had was controlled by Damien. My clothes would cover the body that had been used repeatedly as the release for his violence, as though by dressing it differently I could change its past. But the past can't be changed, and it can never be hidden from, not for ever.

'How often do the two of you talk?' I ask. 'Not about work, not about the kids, not about bills or anything connected to the house. I mean how often do you spend time actually talking about you – your hopes, your dreams, your fears?'

Their answer is evident in the blank expressions upon each of their faces. It's the standard response the question tends to receive. Life entangles people in all its day-to-day complications. It becomes easy to lose yourself, and when losing yourself is easy, losing someone else is inevitable.

Josh looks at me with confusion, a slight smirk playing at the corners of his mouth. 'Do people really do that?'

Next to me, Lydia sighs gently, finding little humour in her husband's nonchalant response. She pushes her fingertips to her eyelids again, her face pinched as though in pain. 'This is what I get, you see. Any time I try to talk to him, really talk about anything, he just makes some flippant remark like that.'

'Josh, can you share with us what Lydia already has, please – how you met, what attracted you to her, what you liked about the relationship in those early days. You were twenty-seven when you met, is that right? So Lydia, you would have been…'

'Twenty,' she says. 'I fell pregnant quickly,' she explains, as though reading some of my thoughts, though she must know I had already worked this out with the information she had provided before they came here today.

'It was the best thing that could have happened,' Josh says quickly, 'but apparently she doesn't feel the same way.'

'That's unfair.'

'True, though, isn't it? If I had a pound for every time I've heard the words "if I could have my time back" ...' He mocks his wife with a cheap imitation of her voice.

Lydia looks at me, that same pleading look in her eyes. 'It's not the same for men, is it? Their lives don't change in the same way a woman's does once a child comes into the picture. I'm not complaining, it's just a fact. But he doesn't realise how hard it's been for me at times. He doesn't understand how lonely I've been.'

I say nothing, knowing there's nothing I *can* say to this. I don't pretend to understand situations in which I've never found myself. I've heard other women, other mothers, make similar comments during sessions, but the kind of loneliness they refer to is an isolation that is alien to me.

'Josh,' I say, remembering that the focus is now supposed to be on him. 'What line of work are you in?'

'I'm a doctor.'

His answer surprises me, though it seems naïve that it should. Doctors, dentists and teachers are no longer the tweed-jacket-wearing men I remember from my childhood. I have met several doctors during my years as a counsellor – both men and women – as well as lawyers and politicians, and even a famous television personality who managed to keep her marital problems hidden from the attention of a media that would have paid a small fortune to get its hands on the story.

'GP?'

'No. Hospital. The hours aren't regular, and they can be antisocial. She knew that from day one, so I don't know why it's suddenly such an issue.'

'Let's go back to day one,' I suggest. 'Tell me how it happened for you.'

'The party or the first date?'

'Either. Up to you.'

Josh stretches one long leg out in front of him, his foot twitching in his brown boat shoes. He isn't wearing any socks; the look is something pulled from the pages of a fashion magazine: the young professional, casual and successful. There is something too try-hard about it, and I wonder who he's making the effort for.

'I met a girl at a bar,' he says, sounding like the blurb of a romantic novel. 'It's not very original, I know, but that's how it happened. She was pretty, we got talking. She mentioned where she worked, so I thought I'd surprise her. We met up that evening and went for a drink. One drink led to quite a few, for her at least. I thought maybe it was a confidence thing, you know, or she was a bit nervous, whatever. Most of us have probably been in that situation at some point, where you're tense and you have a drink to take the edge off. I know I have. I didn't really think much of it at the time.'

Lydia's drinking is obviously an issue here, raised once again by her husband, but I don't want to delve too much into that, not during this first session. Scratch the surface of a problem too soon and it can do more harm than good, though it is a reminder that not everything here may be as black-and-white as it seems. The extent of Lydia's drinking is still unclear, as is the effect it has had on both their lives. I judged Josh quickly, but there are elements to Lydia's character that I believe have also yet to be revealed.

'What did you like about Lydia when you met?'

He looks at her in the same way she not so long ago looked at him, a curious kind of emptiness behind his eyes. I feel an unexpected sadness tug at my chest for this couple I barely know anything about.

Whatever has gone on between them, they both look lost. Though I've worked with many couples during my career, I have only known a few of which this could be said, and I've usually escaped the trap of becoming too emotionally embroiled in the lives and lies unravelled before me. It has happened, but I have tried to learn from it.

'She was nice to look at – I mean, that was obviously the first thing I noticed about her. I didn't know her, so I didn't have much else to go on. Then we got chatting and she seemed pleasant enough. She was very family-orientated – she talked about her parents a lot. I liked that. And she seemed interesting, you know, not like a lot of other girls I'd met. She had interests that were a bit more unusual. That's why I took her to see that play.'

Josh's unyielding reluctance at being here loosens as he speaks; the more he talks, the less hostile he becomes. The change in him serves as another reminder that nothing in this room is ever as it first appears. I have seen acts played out in front of me on many occasions – performances delivered with convincing skill, though nothing has ever come of them other than disappointment – and I know better now than to take anything at face value.

'And you were happy when she became pregnant early in your relationship?'

'Very.' He nods. 'I always wanted a family. Perhaps I hadn't thought about starting one so soon, but I never had any doubt it would be the best thing to happen to us. And it was. I still think it was, despite everything. I love the kids.'

Lydia shoots him a look that is so filled with contempt it takes me by surprise. The way Josh speaks about his children would surely make most wives happy, yet her hands move to the arms of the chair, her nails gripping its sides as though keeping her from falling forward. I cannot understand her reaction; not unless what he says about his children portrays something far different to the relationship she witnesses at home.

But why lie here, to me? I think. People have done so in the past, to save face or to make themselves appear a better partner than they are, but they are lying to themselves too, and wasting everyone's time, mostly their own.

'What do you think has changed, Josh? Over time, how has the relationship altered for you?'

'I don't feel like a married man,' he admits. 'I go to work, I come home, I spend time with the kids, but beyond that, there isn't anything any more. She doesn't talk to me—'

'You don't listen.'

'She drinks too much—'

'You mentioned that already.' Lydia continues to appeal to me for help, as though I might be able to stop her husband raising this issue that she apparently wants to keep behind closed doors, for the time being at least.

'It's almost like living with a friend,' he says, ignoring her for a second time. 'But not even that really, because at least friends get on with each other. I don't know what we have in common any more.'

It seems to me that this relationship is a case of too much, too soon; something I have seen before in this room; something that also applied to Sean's relationship with his daughter's mother. Sienna was born just eighteen months after they met, when her parents were both in their early twenties. They separated before her second birthday, though the relationship remained civil and they worked together to give their daughter a stable and happy childhood, but having a baby so soon into their relationship meant they had little time to get to know each other. I wonder if the same applies to Lydia and Josh.

It takes years to get to really know a person. Sean and I moved in together two years after meeting, and even six months on from that I found myself surprised at the things I was still finding out about him, those seemingly small, everyday things that when seen recurrently come to form a part of someone's character, sometimes without them even being aware of them.

'These things you describe,' I say, 'are very common. Life is hectic – it's probably busier for people now than it's ever been. It's easy to lose each other a bit along the way.'

Lydia is looking at me, waiting for me to wave a magic wand and give a simple, single-sentence solution to the problem. I wish one existed.

'Is that what you think of us?' she asks. 'That we're lost?'

Her tone is so difficult to read that for a moment I wonder whether her words are an accusation. I'm not sure what she wants to hear from me, so I do what I always do in these circumstances: I answer her with a question of my own.

'Do *you* think you're lost?'

Lydia shrugs. 'Maybe. I don't know. Sometimes I'm not sure how I'm supposed to feel.'

'There's no particular way you're supposed to feel,' I tell her, wondering whether that's something Josh attempts to dictate. My first husband would have controlled my thoughts if he'd been able to. Men like Damien Hunter have become easier to identify over the years: they are detached, flawless; they are never to blame for their own actions. Already there are elements of Josh Green's character that remind me of him. 'What I mean,' I add, feeling the need to clarify my point, 'is that there's no rule book. There's no right or wrong to whatever you're feeling.'

'I don't feel lost,' she says. 'I'm exactly where I'm meant to be.'

She holds my eye with an intensity that implies her words suggest more than she can articulate. I wonder what she means by it, knowing that I should try not to read too much into what hasn't been said.

'So how do we start to put things right?' she asks, breaking the silence that has descended between the three of us.

I glance at Josh, who is staring at the clock on the wall. We have just a few minutes of the session left, and he appears to be counting them down.

'Firstly, you need to make time for each other. Proper time. I'm going to ask you to do something for me. Between now and this time next week, I'd like you to go out somewhere, just the two of you. Is there someone who can look after the children for an evening?'

Lydia nods.

'I want you to go somewhere you can talk, so don't choose the cinema or anywhere like that. Pick a nice restaurant, stay there for a couple of hours at least, and talk to each other. Some subjects are off limits: work, the kids, the house, money. Try to avoid mentioning anything that's been said during this session as well, okay?'

'There'll be nothing left to talk about,' Josh says.

'You'll be surprised what you find when you need to look for it, trust me. Is it a deal?'

'Deal,' Lydia says.

Josh nods. He stands from the sofa and reaches out a hand to me. 'Thank you.'

When I take his hand, his fingers squeeze around mine, gently at first and then a little too tightly, his fingertips digging into the palm of my hand. I look up at him, taken by surprise. Our eyes meet, and he smiles; drops my hand as though the moment was completely normal; as though it hasn't happened at all but is merely my imagination. I look away, wondering if Lydia has noticed the awkward exchange.

'See you next week,' he says.

I turn to Lydia. 'I'll get your coats for you.'

They follow me through to the hallway and I retrieve their jackets from the cupboard beneath the stairs. When I turn back to them, Josh's attention is on the line of photographs that need to be straightened. He turns and sees me watching him, his face

impassive as he walks towards me and reaches for the door handle.
He says nothing as he passes me, so I hand the coats to Lydia. He
lets himself out of the house and waits for her on the front step,
the rain having finally yielded to a dry sky and made way for a
struggling strip of blue that is attempting to push through the grey.

Lydia picks up the umbrella they left near the front door and
puts her other hand on my arm, offering me a small smile. 'Thank
you for today.'

'My pleasure,' I tell her. 'Take care.'

As I close the door behind them, I wonder why I added that,
as though I am already sure that for one reason or another she
might need to.

I hear my mobile ringtone coming from the kitchen, so I head
back down the hallway, trying my best to ignore the photographs
and the unsettling feeling they inexplicably evoke. Sienna's name
is lit up on the screen of my phone.

'Hi, Karen,' she says. 'I hope I'm not interrupting anything?'

'Of course not,' I tell her, reassured at the sound of her voice.
Sean's daughter sounds so much like him, the same soft lilt in her
vowels. Though she has lived in Australia for over two years now,
her accent remains untouched. 'It's lovely to hear from you.' I glance
at the clock on the far wall. 'It must be late there?'

'Just past eleven. I've been meaning to call you for days now, but
the kids have a way of putting a stop to my plans. Sorry.'

'Don't apologise.' A feeling I know I probably shouldn't allow
myself to have punches me in the gut, a short, sharp jab that is there
and then gone. This is a pity call, one that will ease her conscience
once it's over and done with, out of the way for the next month
or so. I feel uncharitable for thinking it – Sienna is a kind young
woman, well-meaning – but I know she is only calling to check
I'm still managing to hold things together.

Which I am, most of the time.

'So how are things?' I ask her. 'Is the baby sleeping any better?'

She laughs. 'No. I think he might be a vampire.'

'How much maternity leave do you have left?'

'Only another few weeks. Silly, isn't it? I've been looking forward to going back, but now that it's creeping closer, I'm dreading leaving him. Mum guilt.' She laughs again, but the sound is short-lived and is followed by an awkward silence. 'How are things at your end?' she asks. 'Work busy?'

'Not too bad. I could probably take on a few more clients, but I've got enough for the time being.'

I think about Lydia and Josh, how odd they seemed and how uncomfortable he made me feel. I glance into the hallway, my eyes darting along the row of disturbed frames. Uncertainty creeps through me like a chill, though I know there is no rational reason for it. Despite my mind's attempts to fight it, I am taken back to another place, another time.

I am overthinking things, allowing my imagination to run away from me. Nevertheless, I find myself verbalising my disjointed thoughts to Sienna, letting them escape into the air as though holding them inside me will allow them to fester and grow.

'Actually, I've just had a first session with a new couple. They're nothing unusual on paper, thirty-something, two kids, normal sort of marital problems, but ...'

My sentence trails into silence as I realise that I have no way of explaining this to Sienna. I have no way of explaining it to anyone, not in any way that wouldn't make me sound unbalanced. How can I explain something that makes no sense to me?

'But ...?'

'I'm not sure,' I admit. 'He just ... he reminded me a bit of someone, that's all.'

There is silence for a moment. Sienna is more than likely reciting Damien's name in her head, though she won't bring herself to say it aloud. Even if she did, our thoughts would lie with different people.

'Do you think someone's in danger?' she asks.

'I'm not sure,' I say again. 'It's too early to tell.' I linger over my next sentence, uncertain whether it should be aired. 'Do you remember what happened?' I ask, alluding to a time I don't want to put into words. 'You were just a teenager at the time, I know, but do you remember what I did?'

'You didn't do anything, Karen. It wasn't your fault.'

Her words are well-intentioned and the sincerity in her tone is almost convincing, but I'm filled with a sadness that hurts my chest. Sienna is so loving, so kind, and – where this is concerned – so wrong.

'What's brought all this back?' she asks.

It's never gone away, I think, though I don't tell her this. I can't. She is happy now, living the life she deserves; it isn't fair to burden her with something that has nothing to do with her.

'I'm just being silly,' I say, trying to make my tone as breezy as possible.

'You're a good person, Karen. You were a brilliant wife to my father and you're a wonderful counsellor, just remember that. Think of all the people you've helped over the years.'

Her words cut through my chest, stealing my breath. 'Thank you,' I say quickly. 'Look, I've got to go, my next clients will be here soon.'

I'm lying to her; my next clients aren't due for another couple of hours. It's easier for us both this way: she doesn't have to witness my neuroses, and I don't have to be embarrassed by their exposure.

'Okay, but look, Karen, any time you need me, please just call, okay?'

I tell her I will, though I know the promise is made lightly. When she ends the call, I put my mobile back on the worktop and go out into the hallway, where I straighten each of the eight photographs in turn.

My life is ordered, structured, and that's how it needs to stay.

TWO

JOSH

He hated the room within moments of entering it for the first time, and it fails to show any signs of improvement during their second visit. He sees the pride Karen Fisher takes in the atmosphere she thinks she has created here, and he pities her for her self-delusion. The place is everything marriage so often seems to him to be, showy and misleading, furnished with glossy aesthetics that attempt to distract from the blandness that sits at its core.

Karen has gone to make tea again, her little ritual allowing him time to contemplate the long hour that stretches ahead of them.

'Please try at least to look as though you want to be here,' Lydia says.

'I don't want to be here,' he tells her.

'I can't do this on my own. I need you.'

The plea sounds so pathetic, her voice so whiny, that it sends a ripple of irritation through him. 'I'm here, aren't I?'

He can remember them being happy, even though she has chosen to forget it. A memory resurfaces, one spring day at the seaside. She was cold; he had given her his jacket to wear and she kept it on, worn zipped to her chin, as they ate a picnic in the car, watching the tide roll in and the sand gradually lose itself inch by inch to the sea. They played a game of I-Spy that went on far longer than the three S's for sea, sand and sky should have allowed. They kissed, he is sure of it.

There was laughter. She would deny it now, but he knows it existed.

Karen enters the room a moment later, carrying the tea tray. She puts it on the coffee table before reaching for the teapot and pouring Lydia a cup.

'Are you sure you wouldn't like one, Josh?'

He shakes his head.

She adds milk to her own tea and stirs it, the tinkling of the teaspoon against the side of the cup sounding like the announcement of a speech at a wedding breakfast.

'I think we should talk about what's happened since the first session,' she says. 'How have things been between you?'

'Nothing's changed.' He pushes the sleeves of his sweater up his arms. The heating is on – somewhere in the hallway he can hear the clunk of a radiator that needs bleeding – but neither woman seems to feel the warmth that is filling the room and making him feel sticky beneath the stupid shirt he is wearing. 'I mean, I wouldn't expect it to after just one session, obviously.'

'Did the two of you go out somewhere for the evening, somewhere you could talk?'

'We went for dinner.'

'Great. Where did you go?'

'There's a new restaurant opened not far from us. Italian.'

'And how was it?'

'Great. I had lasagne.' He holds Karen's gaze, wondering what she makes of him so far. He knows he has been flippant; he often finds it hard to be anything else. 'We talked about what we'd done that day,' he says. 'That took all of five minutes. It all got a bit boring after that.'

'And what had you done that day?' Karen asks.

'Work, but we weren't supposed to speak about that, were we? We had to in the end – there was nothing else to talk about. It was all pretty tedious stuff.'

'I can't imagine for a moment that your job is tedious. I'm sure Lydia must find it interesting.'

'Do you?' he asks, turning to her. 'Do you find it interesting, Lydia?' He stretches her name, turning it into a sneer. Karen's eyes haven't left his face; he feels her stare, heavy and concentrated, studying him.

'Of course I do. I'm always interested in your day; you just never ask about mine.'

'I did ask,' he defends himself. 'You just didn't give much of an answer.'

'What was there to say? Every day is much the same for me.'

'And that's my fault?'

'Did I say that?'

'You didn't need to.'

'This is what he doesn't get,' Lydia says, turning to Karen. 'He keeps using the word "boring", but that's what my life is.'

'Must be awful for you,' Josh drawls, rolling his eyes. 'Nice house, plenty of money, all that free time to do whatever you want with. What a nightmare you're living, you poor thing.'

'Have you returned to work since the children have been at school?' Karen asks, ignoring his comments.

Lydia shakes her head. 'It's so hard getting back into employment after time off. Most employers don't take you seriously if you've had more than nine months off for maternity leave, and even then it isn't easy. It's impossible to compete with anyone younger and more experienced.'

'Excuses,' Josh mutters.

'It's not an excuse, it's a fact. I'm not that employable.'

'You don't want to be employable, though, do you? Why work when you can continue to be a kept woman?'

The look that is shared between them is prolonged and uncomfortable.

'Let's go back to the restaurant,' Karen suggests, apparently keen to cut through the mounting tension.

'Which bit?'

'After you'd each talked about your day, what happened then?'

'Well,' Josh says. 'Things just got increasingly awkward after that.'

'What made it awkward?'

An image flits through his brain, fleeting yet as vivid as the sofa he now sits on. Karen is at his feet, lifeless, her brain spilling in bloody tendrils from an open wound that has been carved into the back of her head by his own hand.

'Are you okay, Josh?' Karen asks.

He has self-diagnosed these pictures that often snap into his mind, moving quickly and in stages like those flip books that he used to draw when he was a child: a man running across the pages until a cliff edge appears, and then *splat*, a smear of red ink on the final sheet of white. Intrusive thoughts: he has read about them in psychology magazines, in articles that describe exactly what he experiences and how these images make him feel; how, on his worst days, he is frightened of himself and what he might be capable of.

'I'm fine,' he lies.

'You were going to tell me what made the evening at the restaurant awkward for you,' Karen reminds him.

'I just don't know what she wants from me,' he says, returning to the conversation and folding his arms across his chest. 'Well, I do know … I just don't know if I can give it to her. I don't know if I want to.'

He feels Karen's eyes upon him as she wonders about the meaning of his comments.

'What do you think Lydia wants from you? What can't you give her?'

'She expects me to agree with her on everything, that's the problem. She likes to argue with me a lot, particularly when things don't go her way. That's what happened at the restaurant. I don't need her to tell me what I should be thinking. You don't get it, do you?' he says, his words thrown across the room. 'I've spent years trying to please you, going along with everything just to keep you happy, but coming here and doing this, I'm still not sure it's right. I'm sorry,' he says, as he watches her expression change. 'I'm just saying how I feel. Why can't you be happy just to live your life? Why do you always have to go over and over the past? It's like a scab,' he says casually, looking back to Karen. 'She keeps picking away at it until she makes it bleed.'

'"Expects me to agree with her on everything",' Karen repeats. 'What do you mean by that? Can you be more specific?'

He exhales heavily, trying to expel the tension. He needs to be calm and in control here. 'Just day-to-day things,' he says, waving a hand to swipe the question to one side. 'You know.'

Karen's face says his answer isn't enough. 'You mention the past. What is it you think Lydia wants to keep going back over?'

'It's hard to explain. She wants me to see the world the way she does, but I can't. I won't. She might learn one day that things would be a lot easier for her if she argued with me less.'

He wants to know what Karen is thinking. He imagines tapping into her head, cracking it like an egg with a teaspoon and watching the blood spill like red yolk down the fragile shell of her face.

'Can you give me an example, Josh?' she asks.

He sits forward, puts his elbows on his knees and rests his chin in his hands. He is losing himself in this room and he knows he can't afford to let that happen.

'Let's talk about what really happened in the restaurant,' he suggests, avoiding a direct answer to Karen's question.

'What happened in the restaurant?' Lydia repeats, glancing nervously at Karen.

He raises an eyebrow, knowing no matter how poor her memory is she can't possibly have forgotten this. 'At the weekend,' he says slowly, stretching the syllables as though talking to a wayward and disobedient child. 'You know … what *you* did. How *you* behaved. It was supposed to be a nice evening, wasn't it?' But everything gets ruined when you've had a drink.'

She is crying now, silent tears rolling down her pale, tired face. Karen sits forward and leans to the coffee table to pour a cup of tea, which she passes to her, as though caffeine and sugar hold the solution to all life's problems. He sees blood again, broken pieces of china this time, and he closes his eyes to push the image back.

'It wasn't my fault,' she says, looking imploringly at the counsellor. She sips the tea as though it is a medication for her nerves before balancing the cup on her bony knee, all the while avoiding making eye contact with him. 'I felt so uncomfortable there.'

'What made you feel uncomfortable?'

God, he thinks, all the woman does is ask bloody questions: question after question, each one taking them round in incessant circles that lead nowhere. Is this how it works, that eventually she asks enough questions to make a couple decide that they would rather endure one another than face having to sit in this room for yet another hour of their sorry lives?

'It's what he does,' she says, her voice small and pathetic. 'He makes me feel uncomfortable whenever we go anywhere. That's why I stopped going out. That's why I drink,' she adds.

He feels like getting up from the sofa to give her a standing ovation.

'I know I've got a problem, okay?' she says, finally meeting his eye. 'But have you ever asked yourself why that might be?'

'It's my fault?'

'This is the problem,' she says, speaking to Karen, her voice lowered to little more than a whisper. 'He never sees any fault in anything he does. He never thinks he's to blame for anything – it's always my fault.'

'Let's slow things down a minute,' Karen says, raising a hand in the way a schoolteacher might. 'Josh, if we could come back to you for a moment. You said you feel that Lydia wants you to see the world the way she does. Could you expand on that?'

'The thing with Lydia,' he says, tilting his head to one side and delivering his words in a mocking, sing-song voice he knows will infuriate her, 'is she likes to have things her own way. She's always been the same.' He holds her gaze, drinking in the look she is giving him. *That* look. 'She can't seem to accept that she doesn't need to get her own way all the time.'

Karen is looking at him with pursed lips. 'What do you disagree on?'

He glances to the woman he calls his wife, knowing she is waiting for him to trip himself up in front of the counsellor. 'Her drinking, mostly.' He needs to keep the conversation centred around this topic, if only to save himself from becoming the focus.

'You've acknowledged you have a problem with alcohol,' Karen says, the words leaving her mouth tentatively, as though she is reluctant to delve any further into such a delicate topic.

Lydia nods and wipes the back of a hand over her right eye as though pushing back tears.

'Have you ever sought help for it?'

She shakes her head. 'Well, I did speak to somebody once, a long time ago, but it didn't really help much.'

'Can you tell me what happened at the restaurant?' Karen asks.

She looks up to the ceiling. She wipes the pad of her left thumb along the bottom of her eye, though her tears have already dried. She leans forward to the coffee table, putting her empty teacup beside Karen's. 'Maybe it wasn't such a big deal,' she says, trying to shake it off. 'Maybe it was just one of those things.'

Karen's eyes widen, seeking more from her.

'She got shit-faced drunk,' Josh says, filling in the silence for them. 'She was flirting with the waiter, made a total fool of herself.' He sits back and folds his arms across his chest. 'Remember when the waiter came over with the drinks?' he says, recalling the scene to maximise Lydia's discomfort. He turns to Karen. 'She leaned forward and put a hand on his arm, giggling like some stupid teenage girl. Her chest was practically falling out of her top. She was acting as though the two of them were the only people in the room, like she'd forgotten where we were. What sort of woman behaves like that out in public?'

'I said I was sorry,' Lydia says, her voice like a child's. She turns to Karen. 'I don't know why I did it, it was stupid.'

'How did it make you feel, Josh?'

'Sorry?'

'When Lydia flirted with the waiter like that. How did it make you feel?'

He is annoyed by the stupidity of the question; how pointless it is. 'I was angry,' he says. 'Obviously. Her behaviour was embarrassing. She's too old to be flaunting herself like that – she's a mother, for goodness' sake.'

'Can you try to explain your behaviour, Lydia? Can you tell Josh why you did it?'

He watches her expectantly, wondering where she will go with this answer.

'I don't know. I just … I feel invisible a lot of the time. They say it happens to women after a certain age, don't they – that we just disappear? But I'm not old enough for that yet. Some days I feel as though I'm in my sixties, not my thirties. He never pays me any attention. I'm not ready to disappear, not yet. I just wanted him to notice me.'

'Well that certainly happened.'

'What makes you feel invisible, Lydia?' Karen asks. 'Can you be more specific?'

Lydia glances briefly at him before averting her eyes. 'I don't go out much. I'm always in the house. I'd almost forgotten what it's like to put on some nice clothes and make a bit of an effort.'

'Is that my fault as well?'

They lock eyes for a moment, and he waits for her to look away first. Karen is watching them, gauging the atmosphere between them.

'This isn't about finding fault or blame,' she says. 'It's about finding a way that you can work together to move forward.'

He winces inwardly at the cliché. Could the woman be more of a stereotype?

'Do you think a regular night out together might help?' she says. 'Once a month, even … just the two of you. It'll give you both something to look forward to, something that's not related to work or family life. Time out with each other is important in any relationship. What do you think?'

Lydia is sitting there nodding at Karen as though she is some sort of oracle. Looking at him expectantly, waiting for him to demonstrate an element of enthusiasm.

'Depends how much she drinks,' he says.

She looks at Karen with that same woeful expression she has been wearing like a second skin. 'This is what always happens. He just assumes the worst of me. Any time I suggest anything nice, he throws something in the way.'

Karen sits back and rests her arms at her sides. 'Lydia, do you feel you have a dependency on alcohol?'

'Not at all,' she says with a shake of her head. 'He's making it sound worse than it is. I go for weeks without drinking. It's just that sometimes when I have one, I tend to have a few too many.'

'Alcohol doesn't need to be involved in these nights out, though. You can go out for dinner without either of you drinking, or you can do something else together. There are plenty of options.'

Is this the extent of her relationship advice? he wonders. Go out for the night; forget your problems over dinner. If only life was that simple.

'You don't even have to leave the house,' Karen says with one eye on him, as though she has read his thoughts and is less than impressed with his assessment of her abilities. 'It's not where you are that's important – it's finding time in which the two of you are together without the distractions of other things. Switch your phones off and make sure you get time to talk to each other.'

'We can't talk when it's just the two of us, though,' Lydia says. 'That's why we're here. We need someone else with us otherwise it just ends up in an argument.'

'That's because you never listen,' he says.

She looks away, casting her eyes to the floor in that infuriating way she has. 'I do listen.'

'Listening is obviously just as important as talking,' Karen says. 'You need to learn to let each other speak. Be honest here – do you find yourself sometimes not listening to what's being said because you're preoccupied with thinking about what you want to say next?'

She is looking to him for an answer and the fact sends a flame of anger flickering through him.

'Most people do it without realising,' she says when he offers no response. 'I know it's not always easy, but when you start to listen to each other – really listen and actually take on board what the other person is saying – you will begin to find ways through your problems rather than just skirting around them, I promise.'

He wonders whether she should be making a promise like this: a promise she surely knows has no guarantee.

'If you feel alcohol is causing issues within your marriage,' she continues, 'I could refer you to someone you might want to talk to. I appreciate you're already spending money on counselling, but there are services that offer free advice and support in matters such as this.' She studies Lydia with a small smile, sympathetic to her vulnerabilities. He sees what is happening here.

'Have a think and let me know,' she adds, when the offer receives no verbal response. She clears her throat and turns her focus to Josh. 'What are your thoughts about forgiveness?' she asks. 'Do you feel that the two of you are forgiving of each other's flaws, or do you tend to hold grudges?'

'She can be stubborn,' he says flatly.

'And you're not?' Lydia says, in that small voice that says: *help me*.

He shrugs. 'No more than anyone else.'

'It's one of the things that causes the biggest issues in a lot of marriages,' Karen tells them. 'It's easy to hold on to a grudge, but over time they can become destructive, for both of you.'

'Are we still talking about what happened at the restaurant here?' he asks. 'Because if we are, that was only last week. It's not exactly something I'm dredging up from years back.'

'I wasn't referring specifically to the restaurant,' she says. 'Look, if I can speak openly with you, you both seem very frustrated with one another. Josh, you've made several references to Lydia's drinking. Lydia, you seem to feel that Josh doesn't pay enough attention to your needs. How do you see a resolution to the issues between you?'

'She needs to stop drinking.' He rolls his eyes, knowing that the look infuriates Lydia. He refuses to make eye contact with her, but he feels her attention on him.

'Okay. Well that's something that can be worked on. You've both acknowledged there's an issue, so there's no reason now that it can't be resolved. Lydia,' Karen turns to her, 'what about you? What do you think needs to change within the relationship?'

'I don't know,' she says, opening her eyes wide and looking at Karen earnestly. 'I think maybe I'm expecting too much.'

He sees the flicker of a reaction cross Karen's face, and he wonders what she takes from the comment.

'In what way?'

Lydia hesitates, her mouth moving slightly but no sound escaping her. She looks up and smiles at Karen, shaking her head as though dismissing the thoughts that recently lingered there. 'I don't really know what I mean. Sorry, it's been a lot to take in today.' The colour in her cheeks has risen and she runs a finger under the neckline of her dress to cool herself down.

'Are you okay?' Karen asks.

'Fine,' she says, the answer too quick and too abrupt. 'Just a bit hot and bothered, that's all. Would you mind if we leave it here for today?'

THREE

LYDIA

It never seems to stop raining. It is their third time here, and yet again the sky has closed in on them, swaddling the city in a suffocating cape of grey. It seems forbidding somehow, as if nature is trying to tell them something; as if there is caution etched in the outline of the clouds, visible with only the closest of studies. But even if she sees it, she won't heed the warning. She has never been very good at taking advice, even when it has been needed most.

'I'd like us to start with you today, Josh, if you're happy for us to do so?' Karen pushes open the door of the consultancy room and waits for them both to enter. 'How have things been since last week?'

'No different really.'

'Have you been busy?'

'As always.'

There is an awkward silence in which Karen waits for him to continue, but he says nothing more, allowing the atmosphere between them to fester.

'Lydia, how have you been?'

'I'm okay, thank you.'

'Have you had a chance this week to spend any more time together, just the two of you?'

The question is left open; Lydia looks at him, wondering which of them should speak first.

'Not really,' he says. 'There just doesn't seem to have been time.'

'Lydia, have you considered what we spoke about last time? About possibly seeking some help?' Karen omits the words 'for your alcohol problem' from her question, leaving the elephant to continue its silent stakeout in the corner of the room.

She shakes her head. 'Look,' she says, shifting uncomfortably and avoiding eye contact, 'I know I've got a problem, but we've not been entirely honest, have we?' She looks at Josh now, her eyes urging his to connect with her. 'I know why I drink,' she says, turning her attention to Karen before looking back at him.

He narrows his eyes, a warning.

'We need to mention it.'

He shakes his head. 'It's too soon.'

'It'll have to come out eventually.'

'What will?' Karen asks.

'That's not the cause of it anyway,' he says, pushing the words through gritted teeth. 'Your drinking was a problem way before that happened.'

She gives the counsellor time to absorb the tension between them. She needs Karen to feel it in the way she herself does, though she knows that will never be possible; not this raw, fresh agony she carries around with her every day of her life.

'He was accused of sexual assault. A patient claimed he touched her.'

The words taste wrong in her mouth. They sound wrong to her ears, as though someone else has spoken them. She glances at Karen, whose face has paled slightly beneath the layer of foundation that has been so carefully applied. In this moment, Karen looks as though she is somewhere else; still here in body but temporarily absent in mind.

'Are you okay?' Lydia asks. She leans forward to put a hand on the other woman's arm, a brief role reversal. She allows her fingers to rest on her sleeve, seeking a moment of sisterly solidarity that she suspects will be returned.

She is wrong.

'Fine,' Karen answers quickly and pulls her arm away as though Lydia's fingertips have burned her. 'Josh, perhaps this would be better coming from you?'

'She came in on a Saturday evening,' he says, spitting out the words as though they are poisoning his tongue. 'I don't often work weekend nights, but they were short-staffed that day, so I offered to help out.' He pauses, shifts on the sofa and looks down at his hands. 'That's where being a good guy gets you, I suppose.'

He sits forward and puts his hands between his knees, squeezing them together as though they need to be kept still.

'She was young,' he continues. 'Late teens, early twenties at most. She was with a friend – they'd been out in town for the evening. She said she was having chest pains.'

Lydia sees the way Karen looks at Josh as he speaks, the way her features shift as the story unfolds. Her eyes flicker from left to right, studying him for telltale signs of lies.

'I examined her. It's standard practice. I did everything I was supposed to – there was a female staff member present.' He clears his throat. 'We spoke in the consulting room after my colleague had left.' He raises a hand as though reciting a declaration of truth in a courtroom. 'She was fully dressed at this point.'

'What happened after that, Josh?' Karen asks.

He focuses on his hands again. 'I couldn't see anything wrong with her. I asked her if she'd ever suffered from panic attacks, she said she hadn't, so I sent her away with the advice that she keep an eye on things and go straight to her GP if the same problem occurred again. And that was that, or so I thought at the time.' He pushes his fingertips to his forehead. 'She could have cost me my career.'

'Lydia,' Karen says, shifting position to turn her attention to her. 'Tell me what happened when you heard about the allegation. How did it make you feel?'

Lydia wonders how many times Karen has asked that question in this room, and whether she ever tires of hearing those same six words. 'I was shocked.' She looks at her hands and smiles sadly at the understatement. 'I was obviously very upset,' she adds.

'I didn't do anything wrong,' Josh says, directing his words at Karen as though more concerned with convincing her. 'That girl was a liar. Everyone knew it.'

'The police turned up at the hospital on the Monday,' Lydia continues. 'The girl said he'd touched her after the nurse had left the room … you know, inappropriately. He was arrested.'

He was late home from work, but that was nothing new and there was no reason to suspect that what was left of the evening would be any different to any other. When she heard the front door shut behind him at close to ten p.m., she went to the landing and stood at the top of the stairs. He looked pale and drawn and she could tell from the look in his eyes that his lateness was the result of more than just a busy shift.

An argument followed, angry recriminations delivered between clenched teeth and silences that were somehow more unsettling than any angry words could be.

I didn't touch her.

How am I supposed to believe that after everything else?

Believe what you want. You always do.

That was before the shouting started.

'What happened after the arrest?' Karen asks, snapping Lydia back to the present. Josh still has his head lowered; is still using all his energy to hold back the anger she knows bubbles away inside him every time this subject is raised.

'There was no proof. It went to court, but the allegation didn't stand up. He was found not guilty.'

Lydia waits for the 'how did that make you feel?' question, but it never arrives. Instead, Karen stands. 'Would you both excuse me for just a moment?' She looks flustered as she goes out, leaving the pair of them alone in the silence that sits between them like an uninvited third party. It is short-lived: Josh's anger breaks it, slicing through the air with the speed of an unexpected slap.

'Why did you have to bring that up?'

'She needs to know, doesn't she? We agreed we would talk about it.'

'Not now. Not like this. For God's sake, you can never just leave things, can you?' He is speaking to her through gritted teeth, his eyes narrowed.

She sits back and folds her arms across her chest, shielding herself from his rage. 'Tell me that girl was lying.'

'How many times do I have to say it?' he snaps, his voice low and the words clipped.

'As many as it takes for me to believe you.'

He sighs heavily, then sits back and pushes his hand through his hair. 'She was lying,' he says. 'There. Are you happy now?'

But of course she isn't happy at all. She doesn't believe him.

They are interrupted by the return of Karen, who breezes into the room with a smile that contradicts the haste with which she left just a short time earlier. 'Apologies for that. Okay … Josh. Let's pick up where we left off, shall we? I'd like you to tell Lydia what impact the allegation and the subsequent arrest has had on you, please.'

She waits for him to compose his answer.

'People look at you differently when something like that has been said about you,' he says eventually. 'Even though the case was thrown out, mud sticks, doesn't it?'

'And what about within the relationship?' Karen asks. 'How has it affected you at home?'

'I feel as though I'm treading on eggshells all the time,' he says, studying Lydia's response. 'I feel I have to constantly justify myself.

I'm entitled to get on with my life now. Why should I carry on suffering for other people's mistakes?'

'We keep going around in circles where this is concerned,' Lydia says, addressing her words to Karen. She notices the changed expression on the counsellor's face; the faraway look in her eyes that suggests her mind has drifted elsewhere.

'How much of a recurring issue is this allegation?' Karen asks. 'How often would you say it causes arguments?'

'Daily,' Lydia says.

'What will it take for you to get past it, do you think?'

She shifts in her seat, her eyes cast down to the floor. 'I don't know,' she says, her voice small and almost inaudible. 'If I'm honest, I don't see how we can.'

'Josh can't undo the allegation,' Karen says eventually. 'He's only able to give you his version of events.'

'My *version* of events?' he repeats, throwing emphasis on the offending word. He folds his arms across his chest, his eyes darting between the two women. 'You may as well call me a liar.'

'That's not what I'm suggesting at all.' For the first time in their meetings, it is Karen who looks embarrassed. A flush of pink mottles the top of her chest, quickly chasing up her throat. 'What I mean is that whatever the truth might be, all anyone can do is give their side of it. Whether another person believes them or not is their decision. You can't be punished for someone else's choice.'

'You think I'm punishing him?' Lydia asks, disheartened and frustrated by the suggestion.

'You have to decide what you believe,' Karen says, fighting to regain some control and composure. The flush of colour has risen to her cheeks now, where a red spot sits on either side of her face. 'If you believe in Josh's innocence, you have to find a way to move on from this. That means that once you've discussed it to the point where it's been exhausted, there needs to be no more bringing it back up in arguments or using it to score points.'

Lydia feels herself growing hot with indignation. She had hoped that Karen was on her side. She needs her to be on her side. 'You think he's the victim here?'

'I'm not saying anyone is a victim. What I'm saying is that being here in this room suggests you both want to make this relationship work, and yet when you say you don't think you can get past a particular issue – regardless of what that issue is – it implies that you already consider the marriage to be over.'

Lydia and Josh exchange glances. The silence that follows is broken by Karen, who seems to reconsider her words and the finality with which they have been spoken. 'Allegations such as this are very difficult to move on from,' she says, as though correcting her earlier statement. 'I'm not saying it can't be done – of course it can – but it will most certainly take time.'

'Have you seen this before?' Lydia asks. 'Have you ever known another couple to survive an allegation like this?'

Karen hesitates on an answer, her mouth set in a rigid line as though her face has momentarily frozen. 'I'm not saying it won't be difficult,' she says finally, 'but there's no reason why a relationship can't survive this.'

'But do you know of anyone personally?' Lydia presses.

This time the pause is longer. 'No,' she says. 'No, I don't personally know of any cases. But that doesn't mean they don't exist. If two people want to make something work, there's always a way.'

'I still love him, despite everything.'

'Then there are ways,' Karen says, with a smile Lydia doesn't believe for a moment is sincere. Behind it she suspects she may be thinking something far different. *Get out while you still can.* 'Forgiving doesn't mean forgetting.'

'Forgiving?' Josh repeats. 'Forgiveness for what, though? I haven't done anything wrong. Shouldn't *she* be making it up to me?'

'This isn't about who's right and who's wrong,' Karen says. 'It's about accepting what's happened and how it's affected you both, and finding a way to move on from it.'

Josh tuts and his face lapses into a sneer. 'And how do we do that exactly? Because you keep talking about moving on from this and getting over that, but you never actually tell us how we're supposed to do that. What do you suggest?'

Lydia feels the temperature in the room drop as the two of them lock eyes with one another, Josh's eyebrows raised in expectation while Karen stares him out defiantly.

'Firstly,' she says, her tone cold and stony, 'I suggest you adjust the way you speak to me.'

'This feels like a bit of a witch hunt. I was accused of something I didn't do and now I'm being attacked for it because I expect her to show me a bit of support.'

'No one's attacking you, Josh.'

'It certainly feels like it.'

'I apologise for that. Do you think you might be able to do the same?'

'What?'

'Do you think you might be able to apologise to me for the way you spoke to me?'

Lydia watches back and forth, turning her attention to each of them in turn, hooked by the scene that is unfolding in front of her.

'I'm sorry,' he finally offers. He sounds like a child coaxed into saying the words after being threatened with having his toys taken away from him.

'Thank you,' Karen says, her voice still cold; no gratitude in her tone. 'In answer to your question, what I suggest you do is tell each other exactly how the allegation has made you feel. We've only scratched the surface here today. You don't have to do that in front of me, you don't even have to do it face to face – if you prefer, you could write your feelings down and give them to the other person to read when you're not around. Until each of you really knows how the other is feeling, you'll continue to find yourselves going around in circles. Which way would you rather do it, do you think?'

'Writing,' Lydia says quickly. She looks at Josh, who simply nods in agreement.

'Okay then. What I'm going to ask you to do is write it all down when you get a chance over the next few days, and make sure you read each other's thoughts before the next session. Try to give yourself enough time to absorb them properly before you come back, okay?'

Lydia nods, noticing that Josh doesn't respond. He has been humiliated and won't take kindly to having been made a fool of. She'll pay for it once they get into the car. He stands hurriedly and leaves the room, not waiting for Karen to say anything more.

'Are you all right?'

She meets the counsellor's eye and smiles, doing her best to fix the face she so often needs to wear. 'Of course,' she says. 'I'm fine.'

But it's clear that Karen doesn't believe it. And Lydia needs her not to believe it.

FOUR

KAREN

We need to talk about the children. This is my first thought when I hear the doorbell ring, announcing the arrival of the Greens and the start of what will be their fourth session. Since we met last week, I have found myself thinking about them frequently, their issues concerning me far more than I know I should allow them to. Over the years, I have tried to develop a resilience that might enable me to leave other people's problems outside once the door has been closed on them, in the same way I suspect others in certain types of jobs – doctors, nurses, social workers – must learn to shut their minds off from the tragedies they witness. It is a form of self-preservation.

Though I make the attempt, I still find it hard to switch off from the things I hear. There have been times when these things have haunted me, lingering in the corners of my home and disrupting my sleep. There are people I have met and been unable to leave behind, people whose relationships – and the mistakes I made in trying to help them – are as much a part of my history as my own, but despite all this, counselling gives me a purpose, something on which to focus my limited energies. If I can help these couples, I can get something right.

The news of Josh's arrest and the allegation made against him has preyed on my mind, and I wonder what effect it has had on their two children. They are old enough to be aware of the tensions that have arisen between their parents. I hope for both their sakes they aren't aware of any more than this, but life can be cruel, and children are often forced to grow up too quickly, exposed to a world in which privacy no longer exists and innocence is stolen far too soon. Perhaps their younger child, their son, has been lucky enough to escape the mood that must surely have fallen over the home, though I doubt the same might apply to his older sister.

And what if they are aware of more? What sort of effect must an allegation of this nature against a parent have had on them?

Josh enters the house first, greeting me with a clipped good morning. The tense atmosphere between him and his wife is evident immediately; I breathe it in with the cold air that sweeps into the house with them and swallow it down as though it might offer me some insight into whatever has passed between them in the week since our last meeting. With it, I gulp down a yawn that attempts to escape me. I haven't been sleeping well, though this is nothing new. My life has been plagued by sleeplessness, and this time of year always has the same effect on me, my grey mood reflected in the dark mornings and the evenings that close in before I am prepared for their arrival.

In two days, it will be Christopher's thirty-fifth birthday. Would have been his thirty-fifth birthday, had he been born when he was due to arrive, not the day I first saw his face, when he was forced too early from my body, neither of us ready to meet for the first time.

This time of year always does the same thing to me, sapping me of any will to get up and face the day. The doctor prescribed medication to help with my insomnia, but all it seems to be doing so far is making me forgetful.

'How are you both?' I ask.

Though Lydia and Josh have troubled me, they have given me something to focus my thoughts on, allowing me if only for the briefest moments to escape my memories.

When Josh steps past me, I do what I can to pretend that the look he gives me has gone unnoticed. He is a man who doesn't easily forget or forgive, and he still resents me for the words that were spoken here last week; words he chose to take as a personal attack. How often does he do the same to Lydia? How often does he twist what she says so that he can use it to make her suffer in his silences?

'Okay, thank you,' Lydia replies. It is said automatically and on cue, in the way that a sick person responds 'Fine, thanks' when asked how they are by a doctor, despite fearing something sinister in their symptoms. The irony of Josh's profession occurs to me, not for the first time. It never ceases to amaze me how many people in roles associated with care and compassion seem incapable of these most basic of human qualities.

I wonder if whatever has happened between the Greens since our last session will be shared with me, or if it will be kept hidden. If nothing else, I am certain it is not their only secret. They will have spoken about Lydia's mention of the assault allegation during the last session: how could they not? Josh was angry with his wife for raising the subject, but he surely must have realised it would surface at some point. No secret can stay hidden for ever.

I lead them through to the consultancy room and pull one of the heavy curtains across the window, where a rare streak of sunlight is pouring through the glass in a fiery mid-morning burst of heat.

'Josh?'

He nods but says nothing, as though the gesture is enough of an answer. I already suspect that today's session may be a strained one, particularly if he persists with this demonstration of disinterest. Why pay money to be here if only to then act in this way?

'You've had three sessions now,' I say, as they both take a seat. 'Do you feel the counselling is helping things between you?'

Lydia nods. 'It's definitely helping me. Josh?'

He looks at me in a strange way, with an expression for which I'm unable to find an appropriate adjective. 'We'll see, won't we?'

I decide not to take offence at his words, though the response is both rude and dismissive. His lip is curled in a sneer, giving him an obnoxious veneer that does nothing to help him ingratiate himself, though it occurs to me that he perhaps has no intention of trying to achieve favour with me or, for that matter, anyone else. Lydia glances at him before looking at me, her mouth tightening with embarrassment at her husband's ill manners.

'Have you both managed to do what I asked of you last time?'

Lydia reaches into her handbag and retrieves a sheet of paper, but I raise a hand to stop her before she unfolds it. 'I don't need to see it,' I tell her. 'In fact, it's better that I don't. Whatever you've written there should remain private between the two of you, if that's how you'd prefer things to remain. Have you read it, Josh?'

He nods.

'Was there anything there you weren't already aware of?'

He looks at his wife and nods again. 'There were some things she hasn't told me before.'

'Did it help to write it down?' I ask Lydia.

'Definitely. I think he understands things a bit better now. He's been a lot more patient this past week.'

'Well that's a good thing, isn't it? Josh, how did you get on?'

He shrugs. 'I don't think I wrote anything that's not already been said. She knows how I feel about things.'

'And have those feelings changed at all since reading what Lydia wrote?'

He pauses, studying me while he constructs his answer. 'Not really,' he admits. 'I still feel pretty much the same.'

'And how is that, Josh?' I ask. 'How do you feel?'

'I just wish things were different.' He holds my gaze for a moment, his grey eyes lingering for longer than they should. As with Lydia, his words manage to convey the sense that there is far more behind them, things that have gone unspoken but that long to be said.

'Bear in mind what this exercise has allowed you to do. If you ever find you're unable to tell each other how you feel about something, write it down. It can often be a more effective way of communicating. It tends to result in fewer arguments.'

Neither of them says anything to this. The atmosphere in the room is claustrophobic, and I wish it wasn't so cold outside: if it was warmer, I could open a window and we could all get a breath of fresh air. Sometimes there is something stifling about just being around this couple, although I have no credible explanation for the feeling.

'Would either of you like to share anything that you wrote?' I ask, having gained the impression that Lydia might be keen to share her feelings with me.

I have had other couples carry out this exercise, and it has often resulted in barriers being broken down. Somehow, writing things out is easier than speaking the words aloud, even when later read face to face. Thirty-five years ago, a nurse advised me to write down how I was feeling. With red eyes and an empty heart, I dismissed the suggestion, feeling at the time that I could have gladly stabbed her with the biro she left on the cabinet at the side of my hospital bed. Yet when the ward had fallen silent and the sky outside turned black, I did what she had recommended, allowing the words to spill from me page by page, writing everything I couldn't say to the son I had never met, and everything I wanted to say to the man who had taken him from me.

It was during that night that I chose the name Christopher. I didn't want to think of him as gone, only as somewhere else, imagining he had left me in search of adventure. For over three decades I have continued to think of him in this way, inventing memories of people he never got to meet, places he never got to see, gathering these stories to create some kind of life for the one that was lost.

He would be a similar age to the couple sitting with me now, and as this thought crosses my mind, I find myself having to look away from them both, resentful for a moment that they are here and he is not.

Lydia looks at Josh as though seeking permission to speak. He shrugs, apparently not caring whether she reveals the details of what has been shared between them.

'I told him the truth,' she says, turning back to me. 'I told him that I can't trust him.'

There is an uncomfortable silence. Josh shakes his head slightly, turning his face towards the window, and Lydia looks at her hands in her lap, twisting her wedding ring around her finger.

'Is this in relation to the accusation, or something else?' I ask, the words leaving me tentatively in anticipation of Josh's potential reaction. When she doesn't answer, her husband's voice fills the gap.

'She's just being paranoid.'

And there I am again, thrown back into the past. I am no longer in this room, and it is no longer Josh Green who sits in front of me. I stand before a different man, his voice low and shallow in my ear as he leans towards me, taunting me with his words.

What are you going to do about it?

'What makes you say that, Josh?'

'It's a fact,' he says nonchalantly. 'She's always been the same, always thinking people are talking about her behind her back or trying to make trouble for her. You know, you say you don't get out much,' he continues, turning now to his wife, 'but the truth is, you've pushed everyone away, haven't you? You're too sensitive, that's your problem.'

I feel my jaw tightening as his speech escalates. He is so much like someone I used to know, someone I couldn't stand to be in the same room with.

'I've lost a lot of friends,' Lydia responds quietly, directing her words at me. 'But it's not all been my fault.' She bites her bottom lip and looks down at her lap like a child who has uttered words she fears will get her into trouble. Just how afraid of her husband is this woman?

My heart tightens in sympathy. I was once like her in so many ways; our stories appear so similar at a glance, and yet they are so different. Her children need her, and she wants to save her marriage, whether rightly or wrongly. I wish I could speak with her alone. Perhaps I might one day, but not yet. If there is something greatly amiss in this relationship – as I fear there might be – it is too early yet to go racing in to try to save her.

'It's mine, I suppose?' Josh snaps.

I wait, hoping Lydia will respond to this with something that will allow me a greater insight into Josh's treatment of her. Does he try to control what his wife does and who she sees, and is this what she wants me to realise without her having to speak the words aloud? She says nothing, and her silence is all I expect. With Josh here and his attention fixed on her, she is unable to say what she really wants to.

If Lydia can't speak, she needs me to be the voice that is currently being stifled.

'We've not yet discussed your children,' I say, running a finger along the neckline of my top and trying to shake myself loose from the grip of the past. 'Are they aware of any issues between the two of you, do you think?'

'James is only nine. He's too young to understand what's going on.'

Josh shakes his head. 'That's not true. I think he understands a lot more than you give him credit for.'

'And your daughter?' I ask.

'Lucy,' Josh says. 'She's a real daddy's girl. Nothing will come in the way of that.'

I notice the look he gives his wife when he says this and the tone in which the words are spoken, something smug and satisfied in his delivery. His eyes rest on her face, the corner of his lip tilting in a half-smile that has no kindness in it. Are the children being employed as weaponry in this marriage? I wonder. Sadly, it wouldn't be the first relationship in which I have seen this happen, where a couple use children as tools with which to score points against one another. It rarely achieves anything but acrimony, and the children are inevitably the ones who come out of it worst.

'Lucy is thirteen, you said?'

Lydia nods.

Thirteen is a difficult age, I think. A teenager in number but not yet in maturity, though no longer a child as a nine-year-old still is. Though I have never met the girl, I feel a surge of sympathy for her that pulls at my heart. It is likely that others at her school have heard of the allegation made against her father, and children can be capable of such nastiness when given an opportunity for it. How must this child's perception of everything she has known to be true have been altered by her father's arrest?

'Is she aware of what's happened?' I ask. 'In relation to the allegation?'

Lydia nods. 'She knows what the girl accused her father of. She doesn't believe a word of it; she never has.'

There is something uncharacteristically adamant in Lydia's tone; she is usually so uncertain, seeming to doubt herself and everything she says. I can't figure out which way her words are intended, whether in defence of Josh or in frustration at her daughter for siding with her father regardless of the accusation, and regardless of what Lydia apparently thinks of him.

'Have either of the children had any issues at school as a result of the allegation? Apologies,' I say to Josh, 'but whatever the outcome of the case, people can be very judgemental, and unfortunately children can be cruel.'

'Can't they just,' he agrees. He clears his throat. 'They've both had problems with bullying. James has become a bit withdrawn, but Lucy deals with things quite differently. She can certainly look after herself. She's got into a few fights over it.'

He says this so casually that I'm taken by surprise. He couldn't sound less concerned about his daughter's involvement in violence, whether instigated by her or as a result of self-defence.

'When you say fights,' I ask, 'do you mean verbal or physical?'

'Both. The other person usually comes out of it worse.' He laughs unexpectedly, the sound sharp and forced as it bounces off the walls.

His attitude is all wrong, suggesting he may even encourage his daughter to fight. I study him carefully, wondering just how much of her behaviour he is responsible for. I have always had the attitude that parents cannot be held accountable for everything their children do, but there's no doubt that everyone is influenced in some way by their upbringing, whether for good or bad.

Josh fixes his eyes on his wife. 'I've tried to warn her, though – she won't always get away with it. One day she'll pick a fight with the wrong person and it'll all backfire.'

Lydia is staring at him intently, a flicker of sadness flashing somewhere behind the resolve in her eyes. Is she jealous of the relationship Josh has with their daughter, of the closeness it seems the two of them share? I wonder if he uses it as a weapon with which to wound his wife. I wonder if he does encourage violence in their daughter, and if so, what exactly that says about him.

'She tries to defend her brother,' Lydia says flatly. 'She always has.' She turns to me. 'He's making it sound as though she's got some sort of anger problem, but that's really not the case. She hates injustice, that's all. She sees the trouble James is having and tries to protect him.'

'What sort of trouble?' I ask.

'Bullying mostly.'

'As a result of the accusation, or is this something that was already happening?'

'It was already happening, but after his father's arrest things got worse. Like you said, kids can be cruel. He doesn't really understand what's gone on.'

'I think he does,' Josh says. The words are delivered in that sing-song voice again, the one that is obviously designed to irritate his wife. It seems increasingly likely that the intention behind it is to belittle her, which he appears desperate to do at any given opportunity. There is something petulant about him, like the teenage boyfriends Sienna used to bring to the house sometimes, who would carry a cloud of cheap aftershave into the hallway upon their arrival and leave a trail of disappointment behind them when they left.

'He might think he does,' Lydia says slowly, 'but he doesn't have a clue what's gone on, not really. He hasn't seen things properly, not the way Lucy has.'

'What do you mean by that?' I ask. 'What has Lucy seen?'

'She's heard conversations,' Lydia explains. 'We try to keep them both away from it as much as possible, but she's aware of arguments and she's not stupid. I know she'll have read things as well – we couldn't keep her away from everything.'

'What do you think she's heard, exactly?' Josh challenges.

Lydia sighs and sits back, pressing her fingertips to her left temple. 'That argument in the kitchen.'

'Which one?' He rolls his eyes as he says this, as though the number of arguments that have taken place makes it difficult to distinguish one from another. I wonder if he ever sees himself responsible in any way for them, or whether Lydia takes the blame. Most of the arguments I had with Damien resulted in him accusing me of being paranoid or hysterical. If I got upset about something, I was overly emotional; if I shut myself off and refused to rise to whatever had sparked that particular row, I was uncaring and heartless. Whatever the resolution – on the occasions when there was one – things were invariably my fault.

'She heard us talking about the arrest.'

I look from Lydia to Josh, waiting for one of them to offer some further details about the exchange. 'What do you think she heard?' I ask, when neither says anything more.

Josh's eyes widen as he studies his wife's face, waiting for her to respond in some way. Lydia looks down at her hands, as though it is she who is guilty of something.

'Oh,' he says flatly after a moment, as though suddenly recalling the incident to which she is referring. 'The argument when you said you believed that girl, you mean?'

Lydia's cheeks flush pink. At first the colour makes her look as though she is embarrassed by Josh's words – as though she considers her suspicion of him a source of shame – but then I realise it isn't that. She isn't embarrassed. She is angry. Fury fills her in a burst of mottled red, and her hands have shrunk into the cushion beneath her, balled into fists.

'And this is why we argue,' Josh says, raising a hand and then dropping it: case closed. 'She doesn't trust me. She thinks I'm capable of that, what that girl accused me of … so what's the point of any of this?'

'Did Lucy hear you say you believe the accusation, Lydia?'

Lydia nods. She looks up from her lap and bites her lip, fighting back tears that I suspect are ones of frustration rather than sadness.

'She loves her father very much,' she says.

Poor Lucy, I think. No matter how great her love for her father – no matter how close the relationship between them – there must be at least a part of her that has considered her mother's doubt and questioned whether it is in any way justified. There must surely be a voice in her head, regardless of how small, that asks: *What if?* And what must that voice be doing to her?

'She doesn't believe a word of what that girl said,' Josh reiterates.

'And what about your son?' I ask. 'Has James spoken to either of you about this?'

'James doesn't really speak about much,' Lydia says, finally looking away from her husband.

'He isn't stupid,' says Josh. 'He knows more than you give him credit for.'

'Lucy is a very perceptive girl,' Lydia continues, wiping her eyes and ignoring Josh as though he hasn't spoken. 'She's older than her years in many ways. She sees things a lot of people might miss. I don't know exactly how much she heard, but it wouldn't have taken her long to join the dots.'

My heart swells in my chest for this child, caught in the mess created by the adults in her life. It is in no way her doing, yet she will suffer for it in years to come. But isn't this the result of most traumas children are forced to face? Divorce, separation, abuse, neglect … all innocence is at some point lost to the hands of an adult, whether intentionally or unwittingly. Though I still know so little of her, it seems to me that Lucy is a loyal child whose opinion isn't easily swayed by the judgement of others. If Lydia isn't convinced of her husband's innocence, her daughter's faith in him might be difficult for her to accept.

'Beyond the allegation, how would you describe your relationship with the children?'

They glance at one another, neither knowing which one of them is expected to answer first.

'Lucy and I are very close,' Josh tells me, taking the lead. 'James is a bit distant sometimes, but that's just his way. He's a deep thinker, he always has been. He finds it difficult to get close to people.'

'You don't show him the love you show her,' Lydia says slowly, her words drawn out. 'He obviously knows it. It's the reason he's the way he is.'

Josh's face changes instantly and he looks at Lydia with an expression of sheer contempt. I wonder how often this argument has arisen between the two. I get the impression that the subject isn't new and has been responsible for friction between the couple for some time.

'What do you mean by that, Lydia? "The way he is"?'

She adjusts herself in her seat, her tears now dried. In these past few moments it seems something has changed; she has found a resilience that was not long ago failing her. 'James is insecure,' she says, keeping her focus on Josh. 'He doesn't trust people and he questions everything. He puts on this big performance, trying to make people believe he's tougher than he is, but I see what they don't. He can be flippant, as though he doesn't care about anything or anyone, but beneath it all he's just a scared little boy desperate for his daddy's love.'

Josh slams a fist against the side of the sofa, taking both of us by surprise. 'You're talking shit!' I see her flinch beside me as he stands and goes to the window, his back to us as he waits for his emotion to ease. At his side, his hands are clenched into fists. She has hit a nerve. Is he angry at her misreading of his treatment of their son, or is his reaction based on the knowledge that everything she has said is an accurate portrayal of the situation?

'Josh,' I say, my tone a warning. He needs to control his temper, or the session will be ended. There won't be an invitation for a fifth.

He turns back to us, his face flushed. 'There's nothing wrong with him, or there wasn't until you got your claws into him.'

Beside me, Lydia's face has changed. Her lip is quivering with the onset of tears, and when they begin to escape her, I stand, go to the sideboard and offer her a tissue from the box I keep there.

I stare at her husband long enough for him to read the look. If he knows he has behaved inappropriately, there is nothing to suggest it in the way he looks back at me.

'Thank you,' Lydia says through a sob, putting the tissue to her face.

'Here we go,' Josh says with a roll of his eyes, his tone cruel and filled with venom.

'Josh,' I say sternly, adopting a tone that sounds like that of an exasperated parent. I don't intend it to, but this couple bicker like children and my response seems to come as a natural reaction to their behaviour. 'Let's remember why you're here. If this is going to work, you need to stay calm and treat each other with respect.'

'This is what she does,' he says, frustrated by my apparent siding with his wife. I know this is what he thinks; I've seen the way he looks at me and rolls his eyes whenever I say anything that might be construed as support for her. 'She turns on the waterworks and everyone takes pity on her. I'm always the bad guy, aren't I, Lydia?'

He stretches out the syllables of her name, drawling them as though drunk. That sing-song, taunting tone is back, mocking her. This shouldn't be about taking sides, but if I had to choose, it would be Lydia every time. I see someone else in her. I see myself.

'If you want this session to continue, Josh, I suggest you sit down.'

I expect him to respond with a sarcastic comment; instead, he sits back on the sofa like a reprimanded schoolboy. Lydia is dabbing her eyes with a tissue. I find myself feeling immense pity for her. Josh is volatile and defensive, and it is little surprise that she has found herself unable to discuss their problems with him without the presence of a third party.

'The accusation has obviously put immense pressure on you all as a family, but what you need to remember is that your children look up to you to be the strong ones in this situation. You set the example on this, as with everything else. Do they know you come here?'

Lydia shakes her head. 'We try to keep our problems away from them as much as we can do. It isn't fair on them – James is having enough trouble at school as it is.'

'He hates school,' Josh adds. 'Every day is a battle just to get him there.'

'Is this still in relation to the accusation made against you?'

He shakes his head.

'He's always had problems,' Lydia says.

'He doesn't have problems.'

'He does. The doctor picked up on something before he was even two years old.'

'Picked up on what?' I ask.

'That's bullshit,' Josh snaps, cutting across my question.

'No it's not. It's true. There was always something different with James, even from a young age.'

'Different?' Josh asks, defensively. 'In what way different?'

'You know.'

'Obviously not, that's why I'm asking.'

'It should be obvious.'

'Well it isn't.'

Having spent some time with the couple now, I realise that this tennis match of obtuse comments could persist for some time without my intervention. 'What did the doctor say about your son?' I ask. 'Was he diagnosed with something?'

'Never formally,' Lydia tells me, 'but he made it obvious he thought James might have autism or Asperger's.'

I am unprepared for what happens next. Josh lunges from his seat and throws himself towards Lydia as though he is going to grab her by the throat. The tray is knocked from the coffee table, sending tea and milk splashing onto the carpet. I spring from my chair without thinking – my body responding instinctively with a fight-or-flight reaction – yet Lydia doesn't move. She remains fixed to the sofa, rooted there in fear; not responding either to Josh or to me as I step in front of her. Yet even before I get there, I realise I am not needed. In that split second in which it seems Josh is going to assault her, he changes his mind, his anger either instantly dissolved or immediately restrained in order to keep its true potential concealed from my view.

He opens his mouth to say something, looks at me and holds whatever it is inside himself. His hands are still curled into fists at his sides. Threat lurks in the room, a tangible fourth party, and I am thrown back to a time I do all I can to try to forget. I remember this feeling vividly, as if it can touch me, though it has been years since I experienced it for what was the first and only time.

What are you going to do about it?

I never want to feel again the way I did that day, and it was one of the things Sean was reassured about when I told him of my plans to set up on my own and run my sessions from home. Being here meant I could use his presence as a deterrent, even on days when he wasn't in the house. But Sean isn't here to protect me any more.

Though I have had the thought so many times before, once again it hits me with the force of a blow. His absence deafens me with its silence, its echoes bouncing from every empty corner of this house. I miss Sean with a pain that is physical, and no number of couples seeking my help will replace what has been lost, though I confess to needing them as much as they appear to need me.

The redness that flared in Josh's face subsides and he moves to the window, standing with his back to us. The view of the garden seems to calm him, which was exactly why I chose this room to work from. His fists begin to relax, his fingers twitching as his anger slips away from him. Beside me, Lydia hasn't moved or spoken. I look down at her. Her mouth is set in a grimace, yet the rest of her features are somehow emptied and expressionless. When she looks up at me, it seems as though she might start to cry again.

'Are you okay?' I ask her.

She glances at Josh's back, making sure his attention is elsewhere.

'Yes,' she says, but she shakes her head, her eyes widened and pleading with me.

I reach down and rest my fingers on her cold hand, briefly, just long enough for her to understand that I know what is going on here.

'I'll just get something ...' I gesture to the tea stains on the carpet, and she looks at me and nods. She knows what I am really asking: whether it's okay for me to leave her alone with him. I go to the doorway and turn back. I need to establish some boundaries. Though I'm sure he didn't intend to knock the table and spill the drink, Josh's behaviour today has been completely unacceptable. He has shown a capability for violence; one I now feel certain isn't so well controlled within the privacy of his own home.

I hear Sean's voice in my ear, telling me to stop this now.

'If you want these sessions to continue,' I say to Josh, 'you need to control your reactions. I will not tolerate such behaviour in my home, do you understand me? You show respect, or you leave.'

It took me wasted years to discover that when you challenge a bully head on, they very often back down. The reaction is so unexpected that it catches them off guard and they have no other response to it. I wish I had learned this earlier in life, but what I failed to recognise for myself back then, I am now hopefully able to show to others. That's why I cannot end this here. No matter how loudly I hear Sean's voice drop warnings in my ear, I will not allow Lydia to be the woman who sits in the corner and accepts whatever is thrown at her.

If I abandon this woman now, the past has been wasted and I have learned nothing from it.

He must hear the shake in my voice, but if he does, he shows no signs of it. He turns to me and gestures to the table. 'I didn't mean

...' His sentence fades away and I notice that there is no apology, either to me or to his wife. 'I don't know what happened,' he adds, as if ignorance excuses everything.

'Whatever it was,' I say, 'it doesn't happen again.'

I wait, my eyes meeting his and holding his attention long enough for him to challenge me if he chooses to. He doesn't. Instead, he goes to the sofa and sits down, lowering his head so that he doesn't have to make further eye contact with me or look at Lydia.

'I'll just get something to clear that up with.'

When I leave the room, I wait for a moment in the hallway. They probably realise this time that I am here and that I'm waiting to listen to what they say, but if Josh is aware of my presence just outside the door, it doesn't stop him from speaking.

'Well at least we know now what you really think.'

I wait for Lydia to say something in response, but she doesn't speak. She just sobs again, the sound stifled perhaps behind the tissue she was still clutching when I left the room, and I hear Josh mumble something that I am unable to make out.

I wonder if this couple would have stayed together if they hadn't had children; if she hadn't become pregnant so soon after meeting him. Though I realise things are often different behind closed doors, it seems there is a divide in the house between James and his mother, and Lucy and her father, and at some point it is likely that at least one of the parents initiated this divide in a bid to seek some kind of ascendancy over the other. It is easy for me to believe I would never have used my own child in this way, but I know it's not as easy as that. It would be a simple judgement based on a hope that I would get things right, but I have got so many things in my life so wrong that I know the assumption is naïve.

The image of Christopher, tiny and lifeless in my hands, snaps before my eyes, there and then gone again. It has the same effect on me now as it did all those years ago, emptying me of everything, hollowing me from inside. He would be not much younger than Josh, perhaps married now and with children of his own. How would I feel if he had grown up to be the kind of man who patronises and belittles the person he professes to love? Would I have blamed myself, or would I have held his father responsible for all that he had become?

When I return to the room, I glance at Josh and see the frustration that still plays out on his tautened features. My thoughts stray in a different direction, one I try to avoid returning to. I wonder whether Lydia realised when she met Josh that he had issues with his anger, or if it was something only revealed to her after they were married. It is easy to be misled by someone if the timing is right and they are the kind of person who can spot vulnerability and make it their target. I know only too well how a kind word, a soft touch and the promise of happy-ever-after can overshadow any flickers of doubt that might spark in the darkened corners the mind doesn't want to reach. Had I looked hard enough sooner, the signs of what Damien Hunter really was were there all along. I chose not to see them, believing him every time he said he would change and that things would be different.

No one else makes me like this.

I scrub at the carpet with the wet soapy cloth I brought back with me from the kitchen, trying not to let the silence that has settled over the room drag me back to that place. No matter how hard I rub, it isn't enough to keep me here. I hear those words spoken again in my head as clearly as though they were uttered just moments ago, and I am taken back to that day; to that hospital trolley and those awful incessant sounds: the bleeping of monitors somewhere along the corridor, the distorted distant voices of a television on another ward, the ringing in my ears that was so loud it was painful. And then the nurse's words.

I really am so sorry.

I close my eyes, trying to push the image of Christopher to a place where I can keep him safe. I want to think of him, but not like that; in my mind, he is grown now, living away as Sienna is. He is with his family, happy and successful.

There's nothing more we can do now.

In that moment, the nurse was the person I was most angry with. Was she really sorry? How could she possibly be sorry enough when she had no idea what or how I was feeling? My child had been beaten inside me, stolen away by his own father before I had a chance to witness the rise and fall of his breathing body. And why wasn't this woman doing anything to help? She was a nurse, wasn't she? She was supposed to make things better; she was supposed to save lives. She was supposed to save his.

'I'm going to end this session here,' I say, my head reeling with dizziness as I stand. 'I'll refund you the half an hour.'

'Must you?' Lydia asks, a note of desperation in her voice. 'End the session, I mean?'

Josh is sitting silently on the sofa, looking down at the carpet between his feet like a sulking child. It occurs to me that his behaviour appears surprising considering his profession, although I should know better than to make judgements based on career choices and qualifications. Some of history's most notorious criminal minds were well-educated, successful members of society, able to hide their true selves behind a facade of respectability, and whatever Josh appears to be within these four walls, there is no reason why the rest of the world shouldn't see a completely different man. It wouldn't be the first time it has happened.

Just how much suffering does Lydia endure behind closed doors?

I glance at them both. It doesn't matter how much they might pay me for my time: I won't be made to feel like this in my own home.

'I don't think anything more can be achieved today.'

'What about next week?'

'I'll be in touch,' I say non-committally.

With her husband's attention removed from us both, Lydia meets my gaze. Her eyes are glassy, as though she is on the brink of tears. She holds contact for longer than is comfortable, and just as I'm about to turn away, her mouth moves, her lips forming the shape of words that can't possibly be read as anything else.

Help me.

I feel a wave of nausea roll in my stomach; taste a shock of bitter bile at the back of my throat. Something turns in my brain, an image I have seen so often yet have tried so hard to push away, and I am almost grateful for the interruption from Josh, who stands and presses his fingertips against his closed eyes.

'I'm sorry about today. I shouldn't have reacted the way I did.'

It is a solid performance: he almost sounds as though he is genuinely remorseful. But I have seen and heard enough to mistrust him. He is going to have to work hard to convince me that he is anything other than a bully. I have known plenty of people like him before: I have grown up with them, worked alongside them; married them. I know what Josh Green is.

After what I have just seen, I know that I am needed. I believe that Lydia is desperate for my help; she's just waiting for an opportunity to tell me so.

After the two of them leave, I go to the kitchen to fetch my mobile phone. I unlock it before getting a glass of water and two paracetamol, which I swallow despite knowing they will do little to ease my headache. It is within me, this sickness – there is no painkiller in the world powerful enough to erase it or disguise its existence. I glance at my phone screen, seeing a notification of two unread emails. The first is a circular from a department store I have previously ordered clothing from, and I delete it without opening. The second email has no title and is from an address I don't recognise: violetsky@gmail.com.

I open it, my heart swelling in my chest when I read the eight words that have been delivered.

How do you sleep at night, you bitch?

The glass of water I'm still holding in my other hand slides from between my fingers and smashes on the tiled floor. The sound pierces the silence that has swallowed the room. Ignoring the shards of broken glass at my feet, I scroll the message up and down, but there is nothing more to it than this. Once again, I feel bile rise in the back of my throat. Leaving my phone on the kitchen worktop and the broken glass on the floor, I go upstairs to my bedroom, pull the curtains closed and lie down on the bed. The searing headache that throbs at my temples tightens, and I stare at the ceiling as I wait for the tablets to kick in.

The words of the email have stamped themselves upon my brain, and though I try to find a way to erase them, they remain fixed there, taunting me. Their irony doesn't escape me. I close my eyes, try to nap, but there is no peace to be found. Sienna's assurances circle my head, echoing in my ears. I am a good person, I tell myself. I am a good counsellor.

But no matter how many times I hear the words, I can't believe in them.

I go downstairs and return to the kitchen, retrieving my phone. Before I have a chance to change my mind, I search for Sienna's number, calling her and praying that she will answer. She is the closest thing I have to a family; she understands me better than anyone else does. Though I have acquaintances in London, there is no one I would describe as a friend. After Sean died, I isolated myself from the world, and there were few people who persisted in waiting for me to return to it.

Sienna answers after a few rings, her voice hushed. I remember the time difference; it is past eleven p.m. in Australia.

'Sorry, have I woken you?'

'Ha,' she says, whispering the sound. 'I'd have to be asleep to be woken up, wouldn't I?'

'Baby still not settling?'

'I've just got him off. He's been screaming all evening. Luckily I left my phone in the bathroom.'

'Sorry. I hope I've not disturbed him. Look, we'll chat another time if now's not good for you.'

'No, it's fine,' she says. 'Hang on.'

I wait a few moments until she lets me know she is now downstairs and able to talk in something more than a whisper.

'You sound tired,' I say.

'It's not for ever,' she says, with typically glass-half-full optimism. She was five years old when I met Sean, and she has always been this way. She never sees limits, only obstacles to overcome, finding challenges where many would only see problems. She faced her father's cancer diagnosis with stoicism, focusing on keeping him as positive as possible, rarely speaking of her own feelings or how his deteriorating health was affecting her. 'Is everything okay, Karen?'

I think of the email, of how eight simple words have had the power to throw me so forcibly off balance. I think of Josh Green, and how his narcissism has brought my past back into my home. Sean fills my being, fills this room; his voice resounds inside my head, trying to reassure me that everything is all right.

No, I want to tell Sienna. *Everything is not okay.*

Instead I find myself saying, 'Everything's fine. I just wanted to see how you're all getting on.'

She is happy, and who am I to mar that happiness for her? It's just an email – it has probably been sent to the wrong address by mistake, or is the result of some random prank, and I'm thinking too deeply into things, as I know I am sometimes prone to do. Sienna is on the other side of the world, enjoying a beautiful life with her beautiful young family. Even if something was amiss here, she wouldn't be able to do anything about it. It would be selfish of me to burden her, and what would I be burdening her with exactly? Only my own insecurities, my own overactive imagination.

She talks for a while about the kids, and though I love to hear her speak about them, I find myself unable to focus on her words. My thoughts are elsewhere, trapped in a different room, caught up in a different life.

'Are you okay after … you know. What you mentioned last time we spoke. That couple, have you seen them again?'

'Yes,' I tell her. 'Everything's fine, just me being silly. You know what my imagination's like … runs away from me at times.'

'You sure?' she says, her tone suggesting she doesn't believe me.

'Positive. I look too much into things.'

'Well, there are worse things to be guilty of,' she says lightly.

Her words, though meant in one way, ring in my ears with the sound of something very different. As though realising the impact they have had, Sienna clears her throat.

'Anyway, when are you coming to see us?' she asks, keen to change the subject.

'Soon,' I say, as I have promised countless times already. 'I can't wait to see you all.'

But I know I am probably lying to her. I am not her mother; not her children's grandmother. They have someone else who fills those roles.

'I should let you get some sleep while you've got five minutes' peace,' I tell her. 'Give the kids a cuddle from me in the morning.'

'I will do. Take care, Karen.'

I end the call and put my mobile on the breakfast bar in front of me. The fridge hums in the silence of the kitchen, and I have never felt more alone.

FIVE

JOSH

He doesn't want to be here today. His memories of the last session have circled his mind, keeping him awake at night and interrupting the cloud of other thoughts that contribute to his restlessness. There is something about Karen, something he can't put a name to. He knows that she is alone in this house that is far too big for just one person, and he wonders whether she craves company: a pair of shoes lined up alongside her own in the hallway; a second wine glass sitting on the kitchen table. Another person's limbs tangled with hers beneath the bed sheets.

'Karen,' he says by way of greeting, nodding but avoiding making eye contact with her.

'Would either of you like tea?' she asks.

'No thanks,' he says.

Lydia also declines the offer and Karen hesitates, her routine disrupted and her expression suggesting her job has now been made more difficult: she has now to fill those three minutes that would usually be spent in the kitchen.

'I think we should start again,' she says, taking the chair in the corner. 'Think of this as a second chance, the page wiped clean. We're going to go right back to the beginning again. Tell me about your wedding day.'

Josh shrugs and tries to focus his mind on something constructive. 'It was a church wedding. She wanted a church wedding, the whole white dress and veil thing, so that's what she got. There were guests. A cake. Bad dancing.' He shrugs again, knowing his response is limited.

'Lydia,' Karen says, seeming to realise that that's the most she's likely to get from Josh. 'What's your best memory of that day?'

He glances at her, sitting there on the sofa and basking in the memory of the wedding, a lavish affair for which little expense was spared. She has everything, yet she appreciates none of it. 'It's a wonder she can remember,' he says. 'Knocked a few back that day, didn't you?'

'Lydia,' Karen prompts her, ignoring what has been said.

'Signing the register,' Lydia says, having had time to carefully consider the answer. 'There's something so official about that part, isn't there? No going back then.' She laughs nervously, and the sound seems to bounce around the room, hitting each of them as it passes.

'Why am I not allowed to mention Lydia's drinking?' Josh asks, fixing his eyes on Karen. 'The allegation made against me was discussed in quite some detail, yet every time I mention her drink problem, you seem to gloss over it or change the subject.'

'Lydia has acknowledged she has an issue with alcohol,' Karen reminds him. 'It has been discussed.'

'Do you remember that barbecue at the neighbours?' He addresses Lydia, ignoring the fact that Karen has responded to him.

She shakes her head.

'Liar. You must remember it. You got smashed, and when I suggested we go home, you caused a scene in front of everyone. Yeah,' he adds, watching her face change. 'You remember now.' He turns back to Karen. 'I've never been so embarrassed. It was the first time I really saw her drunk. She could barely walk, and the more she had, the louder she got. We'd never been invited over to any of the neighbours' houses before. Funnily enough, we never got invited again.'

'Is this relevant?' Lydia asks quietly.

'It is if we're going to get everything out in the open and do this properly.'

'It was years ago. I can't change it and I don't see how it affects anything now.'

'It affects everything now,' Josh snaps, raising his voice. 'If you're only giving half the picture, we're never going to agree on anything.'

A silence descends on the room. Lydia chews her bottom lip while they wait for her response. Eventually Karen speaks.

'There was a reason I wanted to focus on your wedding day. What you both need to do is try to remember the way you felt on that day. There are obviously a lot of unresolved issues here, but the things you loved about each other back when you got married still exist – you just need to find a way to recapture those feelings. They're not lost – they just get misplaced sometimes in the reality of everyday life.'

She is smiling at Lydia as though this is everything she wants to hear, but what Karen doesn't realise is that Josh can see what lies beneath the smile. There is an unspoken dialogue between them, and despite the silence of the conversation, he knows exactly what is being said. *Leave him. Get out before things get any worse.*

'Lydia, I'd like you to list the three best qualities Josh had when you got married.'

'He was kind,' she says, the smirk slipping from her face. 'That was the main thing, I think. He made me laugh. And he was a good cook.'

'And what do you think has changed for you since that day?'

'I'm still a decent cook,' he says.

Lydia laughs nervously and picks at a fingernail. 'Honestly?' she says, as though she is scared to reveal her true feelings. 'Almost everything has changed.'

Karen shifts in her chair. The movement pushes her skirt up and Josh notices a ladder in her tights that runs up the side of her thigh. 'Let's start with the kindness,' she says, tugging at the bottom of her skirt so that it now rests at her knees. 'In what ways do you feel Josh has become less kind?'

'He used to have time for me. We used to talk, but now I'm just there. I do his washing, iron his clothes, cook his meals. I'm a glorified maid.'

'You used to like doing those things.'

'No I didn't,' she protests. 'I've never liked doing those things – nobody *likes* doing those things. I used to do them because you did things for me – you supported me in other ways, so I did what I could to support you. But all that's changed now. There's nothing given in return, you just take what you can.'

He turns to look at Karen, his grey eyes scanning her so quickly she might miss it if she isn't concentrating. 'Ask me,' he says, the words delivered with the tone of a demand. 'Ask what's changed for me.'

'I think you need to address Lydia's concerns first.'

'I don't *need* to do anything. What I'd *like* is to be given an equal opportunity to speak, but that doesn't seem allowed. There's a definite imbalance here, don't you think?'

Karen's lips purse. 'For someone who was sorry for his behaviour last time, the apology hasn't lasted long.'

The air in the room turns cold with her frostiness.

'I don't think I'm unkind,' he says, relenting to the pressure of the stares being delivered by both women. 'I'm busy. Sometimes my tiredness might be misjudged, but that's hardly my fault.'

'Nothing's ever your fault,' Lydia says, her voice small.

'I don't cook any more for the same reason,' he continues, with what he realises must sound like rehearsed lines. 'I'm at work all hours. I'd love to be able to swan around the house all day baking, but someone's got to keep the roof over our heads.'

'That's what I do all day, is it? Swan around? This is where he's changed,' she says, turning to Karen. 'He just takes me for granted.'

'And that doesn't apply to you, does it?' He cuts in before Karen has a chance to speak. 'Let's talk about what's changed with you. The vows have certainly changed, haven't they, Lydia?' He rolls her name from his tongue, unable to keep his sarcasm suppressed. 'You know the ones – you repeated them all, didn't you? The ones about loving each other and remaining faithful for as long as we both shall live. Remember that?'

'I remember,' she says, defiant. 'I meant every one of them.'

'What about you, Josh?' Karen says, in an obvious attempt to soften the increasingly tense atmosphere. 'Can you give me three qualities that you most admired in Lydia?'

'She was loyal,' he says, keeping his eyes on his wife, doing everything in his power to make her uncomfortable. 'She was honest. She seemed to have a strong sense of right and wrong.'

He isn't expecting what happens next. Lydia smiles and moves closer to him, sliding along the sofa and tilting her head to the side in a way that to anyone else might look flirtatious.

'You need to stop this, darling,' she says. She turns to Karen. 'I still love him.'

She slips her hand into his and he looks down at their interlocked fingers, finding himself disgusted by the feeling of her skin against his; by the cold touch of her wedding ring. He pulls away from her, retracting his hand as though her skin might in some way infect his own; not caring what either of them chooses to make of his reaction. Then her hand moves to his leg and rests upon his thigh, and he knows there is nothing he can do about it, not after last week's outburst.

'I've always loved him,' she says, and her fingers tighten their grip on his leg before she pulls away from him.

He moves along the sofa, widening the distance between them.

'Like I said,' Karen says, looking awkward at the unexpected show of physical affection that Lydia has put on for them, 'these feelings aren't lost, not completely.' She smiles at him, but there is no warmth in the look. She clearly knows that Lydia's gesture was forced, and the smile is almost accusatory. *I see you*, it says. *I know what you are.* 'I don't think you're being entirely honest with me,' she adds.

'What do you mean?' Lydia asks.

'Exactly what I say. I get the impression there are things being left unsaid, and if you're not honest with me then you're not really being honest with yourselves. I can't help you unless I know everything.'

Glances are passed between the three of them in a moment of exchange that is long and uncomfortable.

'Josh, is there something you'd like to say?'

'No,' he replies with a shake of his head. 'I've said everything I want to say for today.'

Waiting for Karen to test him, he looks at Lydia, who has fallen into silence at the other end of the sofa.

'I can't stress enough just how important it is that you're both honest in this room. You are paying me to help you, but I can't help you if I'm only getting half the picture.'

Her words, he is sure, are meant for him, yet it is Lydia she is looking at; it is Lydia she is exchanging further silent dialogue with.

'I've been honest with you,' Lydia says, which he realises is as good as saying, 'He hasn't been honest with you.'

'Are we done?' he asks.

'If there's nothing else you'd like to discuss today?' Karen looks at each of them in turn, waiting for one of them to utilise the ten minutes remaining. Neither of them takes up the offer.

They exchange forced phrases of gratitude and less than friendly farewells, and neither speaks to the other before they get into the car.

'What the hell were you playing at?'

'What?' Lydia starts the engine and revs the accelerator unnecessarily.

'Holding my hand in front of Karen. Don't touch me like that again. This isn't a game.'

'I'm aware of that.'

'I know what you're trying to do.'

'Well I'd hope so,' she says, pulling away from the kerb. 'That's kind of the point.'

He swallows down the hundreds of words he would like to say to her, knowing that not one will embed itself between her ears.

SIX

LYDIA

Lydia isn't sure she wants to be married any more. She can't say it aloud to anyone – not even to herself, really – but coming here week in and week out has served to highlight the problems in her marriage, things she has tried to brush to one side and ignore but which she now realises are far worse than she had previously suspected.

'... to help you make this work.'

Karen has just finished saying something; Lydia realises she hasn't heard a word of what has been said.

'Are you okay?' Josh asks, as though he cares. 'You weren't listening, were you?'

She hears the accusation in the question.

'Ironic, isn't it?' he says, firing the question at Karen. 'Apparently I'm the one who doesn't listen.'

'I was thinking,' Lydia says defensively. 'Isn't it just as important to think before you speak, to avoid saying something stupid?'

'Like me, you mean?'

'I didn't say that.'

'You didn't have to.' He looks at Karen and smiles with one corner of his mouth, raising his eyebrows as though to say, *You see ... this is what I've got to put up with.* There is flirtation in the expression, she is certain of it.

'Josh was just saying that he's enrolled on some anger-management classes. I think it's a great idea and a really positive step forward, don't you, Lydia?' Karen looks at her and smiles, but no light shines behind her eyes when she does so. And now she sees it. Karen is playing along with Josh, saying the things she thinks he wants to hear.

'Have you? You didn't say.'

'I did – I told you in the car after we left here last week.'

'No, you said you were going to, that's not the same thing. I didn't realise you'd actually signed up to them.'

'Well, aren't you happy?'

'Should I be?'

He sighs loudly and his fingertips dig into the cushions at his sides. 'There's no winning with you, is there?'

'I just wonder why you've left it so long.' This is true: Josh has needed help for far longer than he would ever admit.

He throws his hands in the air. 'There we are,' he adds, directing the comment to Karen. 'That's exactly what I'm talking about. If I don't do anything I'm wrong, and when I do something I'm too bloody late anyway.'

'Josh has got a point there.'

'Thank you,' he says, though there is no gratitude in his tone. 'At least someone is interested in how I feel.'

'We all know how you feel,' Lydia says with a sigh. 'We've all been listening.'

'Karen might have been,' he says. 'You haven't.'

'You keep saying that, but I have. I know you think I'm ungrateful and that I don't appreciate you, but what about everything I've done for you over the years?'

'Like what?'

'Like just about everything. I've given up my life for you – where would you be now if it wasn't for me?'

She is aware of Karen's questioning eyes on her, but everything she says is true. She has made more sacrifices for him than the counsellor could ever know.

'It's not me who's different,' she adds, unwilling to let the point drop just yet. 'You're the one who's changed.'

'How?'

'You just have. You never used to be like this.'

'Like what, though? You're being a bit vague, aren't you?'

'So controlling,' she says, the words hushed into little more than a whisper. 'You never used to argue with me about everything.'

'You never used to want to be right about everything, that's why. I'm not the one who's changed. You've not been yourself, not for a long time. Ever since Mum died—'

There is a sharp intake of breath; too late, Lydia realises it has come from her.

'Her death was difficult for the whole family,' she says quickly, turning to Karen, 'but he uses it as an excuse for his behaviour. We've all lost people we love, haven't we?' She meets Karen's eye. 'We can't use it as an excuse,' she adds.

'What were you going to say, Josh?'

'Sorry?'

'You said "Ever since Mum died", but you didn't finish what you were saying.'

'Lydia's been different since then, that's all.'

'He's trying to look for something to pinpoint,' she says, knowing she is talking about him as though he isn't there. 'But life's not that straightforward, is it? He wants to be able to look back at a time and say, right, that's where everything went wrong, but I know we won't find it. It's been a gradual decline, you know?'

'I'm sorry for your loss,' Karen says, sounding like every cliché Lydia has ever heard. 'Had she been unwell?'

Josh looks at Lydia before answering. 'I think she'd been ill for quite some time, but she never let on. She was proud like that – she wouldn't have wanted us to worry. She kept everything bottled up, didn't she?'

'Are you in agreement that your relationship changed following the death of Josh's mother?' Karen asks.

Of course they are, she thinks: that, at least, is one thing they are able to agree on.

Josh is the first to respond to Karen's question. 'She's in agreement if she's honest with herself.'

Lydia nods. 'I know it changed the relationship. It changed everything. But that doesn't mean it's all my fault.'

'You didn't care.'

'That's not true,' she argues, appealing to Karen. 'I did care, but he just shut himself off. No one could go near him for a long time, not without being attacked in some way.'

She chooses her words carefully, knowing what they imply. Karen can't have forgotten Josh's potential for violence.

'I took her death hard,' he says. 'I never hid the fact and I couldn't do anything to help that. But she just acted as though nothing had happened, as though we could just carry on with our lives as though Mum had never been a part of them.' He is talking to Karen now, spilling his thoughts in the space between them as though Lydia isn't taking up a part of it; as though she isn't there at all.

'Have you ever spoken to anyone else about this?' Karen asks him. 'A grief counsellor, perhaps?'

He shakes his head.

'Why do you think the death caused a change, Lydia?'

She notices the way Josh reacts when the question is put to her, as though he's the only person who should matter. 'I don't know,' she says quietly. 'I wish I did, then we might be able to put it right.'

He shakes his head, his mouth twisting at her words. 'You're unbelievable.'

She looks at Karen pleadingly. 'We didn't have the closest of relationships, but that's not unusual, is it? Lots of families have tensions.'

'Tensions?' he repeats. 'You never liked her. It was obvious to everyone you never respected her, and you never even tried to get closer to her.'

'It wasn't for me to try.' She pauses; she knows she sounds increasingly insensitive. 'Look,' she says, speaking to Karen. 'She wasn't the easiest of women to get along with. I always wanted to be closer to her, but she tended to isolate herself. She never made the effort and she made it difficult for people to get close to her. I wish I could go back and change things, but I can't. Nobody can.'

'Would you, though?' he says, speaking to her as though he has somehow managed to forget that Karen is there in the room with them. 'If you could go back and change things, would you?'

'Of course I would,' she snaps, trying and failing not to sound defensive. 'Wouldn't you?'

Karen is watching the two of them intently, her eyes moving from side to side as she follows the exchange. She shifts in her seat and moves her attention to him.

'What about you, Josh? What do you feel has changed in the relationship since your mother's death?'

He looks down at his hands. Lydia's eyes linger on his fingers: he isn't wearing the ring she gave him.

'I think it made us both look at things differently.'

Karen says nothing, waiting for him to offer more.

'It did change me,' he admits. 'I disappeared for a while, in a sense, but I don't think that's unusual, do you?'

'I think it's entirely normal and completely understandable,' Karen says, and she is looking at him in a way Lydia hasn't seen before, with a sympathy that has been offered to her but has never previously been extended to his side of the room. 'Grief is powerful and unpredictable. There are no rules for it.'

She feels pushed to one side by the turn in the conversation. 'I understand why he wanted to shut himself away from everyone,' she says, feeling the need to defend herself. 'I did the same when my father died.'

'It's not a competition, Lydia,' he snaps.

'Look,' Karen says, raising her palms in a peacemaking gesture. 'We can't compare one another's grief – it's unrealistic, and it won't help anyone deal with their own. If possible, what you need to achieve is some common ground, a way you can share your experiences and use them to help one another.'

'He thinks his mother's death didn't affect anyone else, but it did. Lucy took it particularly hard. She might not have shown it, but that was just her way of coping.'

'I don't think Lucy was affected,' he argues. 'They were never close.'

'It's not as simple as that. Lucy doesn't always show her feelings,' she tries to explain. 'It doesn't mean they're not there, though.'

No one else speaks, as though they have both been silenced by their misunderstanding of her reaction.

'Lucy would love to have been closer to her,' Lydia tells Karen, 'but she was always made to feel like an outsider.'

'In what way?' he challenges.

'James was always her favourite. He didn't need to do anything to merit it – that's just the way it was.'

'You can't give an example, though, can you? You make these claims, but you've got nothing to back them up with.'

He waits, but she offers no response.

'Well?' he says.

'Her birthday. You must remember Lucy's eleventh birthday? Your mum didn't remember it, though, did she?'

He is looking at Karen with that expression he wears so well, a sneer on his lips and a demeaning laugh behind his eyes. 'It was just a birthday. And there was a lot going on at the time.' He turns back to her. 'You know there was a lot going on.'

She holds back what she wants to say, fearful that if she allows herself to lose control, she will say too much and lose everything. 'She never forgot James's, did she?'

Josh sighs. 'She loved them the same,' he says, looking up from his hands. 'She always did. Whether you chose to see it or not is your problem.'

'Is this something that Lucy has spoken to you about?' Karen asks.

They answer at the same time: Lydia replying with a yes, Josh with a no.

'Please take these words as they are intended,' Karen says. 'Josh's mother is no longer here. Regardless of what either of you may have felt towards her, how she behaved can't be changed now. This is another thing you need to draw a line under, which may mean agreeing to disagree. I'm sure she wouldn't want to see the two of you falling out with one another in this way. If anything, I'm sure she would want you to be happy.'

'She told you that, did she?' Josh says coldly.

Karen's eyes widen.

'I'm sorry,' he says, putting a hand to his forehead. 'I didn't mean that. I shouldn't have said it. I'm sorry. I still find it hard to talk about her.' He stands and goes to the window, looking out onto the garden with his back turned to the room.

'You really might want to consider grief counselling,' Karen says. 'I know it's hard, I really do. There are issues here that will keep recurring if you don't resolve them properly.'

'No one can bring her back,' he says, still looking out through the window. 'It can't ever be resolved.'

Karen looks as though she is beginning to feel sympathy for Josh, but Lydia can't allow this to happen.

'You know when you had us write things down, about how the allegation against Josh had affected us both?' She waits for Karen to nod. 'Well, I was just wondering if … Do you ever offer sessions with just one person?'

Josh turns from the window and looks at her questioningly. Realising what she wants, he shakes his head at the suggestion. 'Anything you want to say, you can say in front of me.'

'I know that, it's just …' She chews the edge of a thumb. 'I can't really, though, can I?'

She waits for him to argue with her, but he doesn't. Instead, he moves from the window and sits back on the sofa. 'Do what you like,' he says with a shrug.

'Is that okay with you?' she asks Karen.

'Of course, if you think it will benefit you.'

'I think it will definitely benefit me.' She smiles gratefully before turning the smile on Josh.

SEVEN

KAREN

I am saying goodbye to a couple I have met with this morning for the second time when I see Josh walking along the pavement just a few doors down from my house. There is no sign of Lydia. I think about going back inside, closing the door and pretending I haven't seen him – ignoring the doorbell as though I'm not at home – but it is too late for that: he has seen me. This is an unscheduled visit; we have planned for Lydia to visit me alone, but Josh gave no indication that he wanted the same. Suspicion creeps through me like a chill. What is he doing here?

The email I received a fortnight ago is still at the front of my mind, its limited contents enough to make my sparse sleep even more unsettled. Is Josh responsible for sending it? It makes no sense that he might be in some way involved; try as I might to work out what his intentions may be, I am unable to fathom how the message is relevant. The word 'bitch' seems so personal, so driven by hatred. He doesn't know me well enough to despise me with such a passion.

He steps onto the driveway and approaches me casually, as though it is perfectly normal for him to be here without his wife. As he nears, I notice how different he looks. He is dressed far more casually than usual, in tapered running trousers, trainers and a black zipped hoodie, and he is clean-shaven, taking years off his already youthful face. The thought that he will want to come into the house fills me with unease, so I begin prepping my excuses for keeping him out here on the doorstep.

'Josh. I wasn't expecting you today.'

I don't know why I say this: he knows I wasn't. He shoves his hands into his pockets and shifts from one foot to the other, not meeting my eye. He seems uncharacteristically nervous, and I am struck yet again by the mess of contradictions this man appears to be. Each time I think I have worked him out, something new about him arises, knocking any previous character assessment off balance.

'Can I come in?'

I remind myself not to be too confused by him. His contradictions are evidence of an act, and increasingly I believe that there are two of him: the version of Josh here in front of me now, and the one who exists behind the closed doors of the couple's home; the one I have seen glimpses of during these past couple of weeks. There are those who can keep their true selves hidden from the outside world, but I don't believe that Josh is one of these people. He may have done well up until now, but the mask will slip at some point.

'I have clients coming in half an hour,' I lie. The truth is that my next appointment is not for another two hours, but if I encourage this unscheduled visit then I run the risk of unwittingly inviting others. I have been nursing a particularly aggressive headache all morning, one I had hoped I might be able to sleep off before my next clients arrive. The prescription I was given to help me with my insomnia hasn't done a thing to benefit my night-time sleep, yet where the days are concerned, I could easily catnap whenever and wherever I find the opportunity.

'That's fine. I can pay you for your time.'

The promise of a nap is snatched from me; it occurs to me that no matter what excuse I make, Josh is intent on coming in. I wonder if this is about his mother. There are issues here that I don't believe he has ever addressed, but if he wants to give his marriage any hope of survival, he is going to have to find a way to deal with the things it appears he has tried to push to one side. Though Lydia's views on the woman appeared unexpectedly insensitive, it is obvious Josh is still grieving, and not everyone is equipped to deal with living with someone who is struggling like this. Not every relationship can survive a loss that is felt so keenly.

I'm not sure what Josh wants from me. I'm not a grief counsellor: that requires a whole different set of skills, ones I don't possess. Since losing Sean, the last thing I feel I can bring myself to do is to listen to the pain of someone else's grief. It is still too raw. I know it always will be.

'This isn't about money, Josh. Look ... what we spoke about last time ... I really think you should consider it. I'm not a grief counsellor. I wish I could help you, but you need someone who's an expert in this area. I can put you in contact with somebody.'

He shakes his head. 'It takes a long time for me to trust someone – I can't talk to a stranger about it. Please, Karen. I don't want to do this in front of Lydia – she doesn't understand.'

I remember this feeling well. When Sean died, it seemed to me that nobody else appreciated what I was going through; that nobody could possibly begin to imagine the weight of loss that I was dragging around with me every day, all the while plastering on a fake smile and dropping empty phrases such as 'I'm fine, honestly' into conversation; words that spared other people the awkwardness of having to try to find a way to cope with my misery. There were no children to share those painful weeks and months with; no family to help break the awful silence that fell over my days. Sienna was suffering her own loss, which I knew was completely different to mine, and she had her own family to think about: a young daughter who needed her attention; her mother to support her through her grief.

'I wish I could help you, Josh,' I say again, and there is an element of truth in my words. Despite everything I suspect of him, no one has a single side to their character. I've seen enough of Josh to believe there is good in there, kept hidden behind the nonchalance and the hostility. There is goodness in most people, though in some it is harder to find. True evil only occurs where there is no goodness at all. I have met with evil in my life only twice, experiencing it once with Damien Hunter and for a second time in the husband of a woman I tried to help. Any trace of goodness in these men was merely a mask for the cruelty that lay hidden beneath it. They were both ruthless and without remorse, and no matter what Josh might be – regardless of the characteristics he might have demonstrated during his sessions with Lydia – I don't believe he is a match for either of these people.

He doesn't say anything, but he doesn't move to leave either. He is still looking down, shifting from side to side, and then his hands come out of his pockets and he is staring at them, working the fingers of his left hand across the palm of his right as though trying to massage out a pain. I think for a moment about the accusation made against him – about what those hands are apparently guilty of – then try to remind myself that he was found innocent. It hasn't been easy to dismiss the knowledge from the front of my brain, where it has rested as though the experience is mine and not his.

He looks at me as though he is about to speak, but then does something I am unprepared for, something I never would have expected of him and am not sure how to deal with. Standing on my doorstep, Josh starts to cry. His tears escape him in a sudden rush that appears to take even him by surprise, and he looks away from me, embarrassed by this show of emotion. I find myself responding in the same way, checking either side of me to make sure none of the neighbours are around to witness what is unfolding.

This is London: people pass each other daily without ever really taking notice of what anyone else is doing, too busy with their lives to ever pay much attention to those of others. Usually I am grateful for this, though it strikes me sometimes that should something ever happen to me – if I was to die in my sleep one night, alone in bed – there would be no one to notice anything amiss. I could lie here, just beyond the locked front door, with no one aware of my need for help. It would be so easy to be the same as everyone else, to turn a blind eye and pretend I haven't noticed the scene that is unfolding in front of me, but if I do that, what exactly does it say about me? Ignorance is the easy option, but it is rarely the best.

With the echo of Sean's voice still in my ear, I step to one side to allow Josh into the house. I am not a fool – I have seen too much and experienced enough darkness to know when someone is playing a role – and though I remain uncertain of who Josh is, I need no convincing that this show of emotion is a very real one: one he seems embarrassed by, almost ashamed of. I know what it is to grieve, and I understand the way this particular kind of pain takes hold, vice-like, until it feels as though the lungs are being squeezed and breathing is impossible. There is so much of Josh I fail to comprehend, but his grief for his mother is at least one part of his character that I am able to empathise with. And if I start with this, perhaps it will open a path for me to get closer to what is happening with Lydia.

He stands in the hallway as I close the front door. When he looks away, glancing down towards the consultancy room in expectation of being taken there, I reach to the drawer in the hallway table and retrieve my mobile phone, slipping it into my pocket. Should I need it, help is just a phone call away. I think of that email, repeating a reassurance in my head that convinces me Josh cannot be involved. I believe it. Though doubt about his behaviour is rooted firmly in my brain, the email doesn't seem like something he would do. If he wanted to call me a bitch, I imagine he would be more likely to do so to my face.

He waits for me to lead the way. When I push the door open, standing back for him to enter before me, he is wiping his eyes with the back of his hoodie sleeve as though attempting to hide any evidence of the tears I have already seen. I think about his outburst here during our last session, of how he seemed so close to hitting his wife. I remind myself not to forget the incident, though it would take far more than a few tears for me to erase the memory of his potential for violence.

'I'm so sorry,' he says. 'How embarrassing.'

'There's no need to be embarrassed.' I follow him into the room and gesture for him to take a seat. I feel sure that once he has composed himself, he will be keen to get away from here and will return next week as though nothing happened, having failed to tell his wife that he came here alone. He is certainly not the type of man who will admit to having been reduced to tears in front of a woman who is little more to him than a stranger.

'Here.' There is a box of tissues on the sideboard; I take one and pass it to him. He accepts it silently, wiping his eyes dry before putting the tissue into his pocket.

'Thank you,' he says. 'I'm sorry. I feel like such an idiot. She gets so frustrated by my grief, I feel as though I'm not allowed to talk about it. This is what I meant when I said she expects me to agree with her on everything. If she's okay about things, I'm supposed to be the same.'

I think about the way Lydia reacted to Josh's first mention of his mother's death. She seemed so cold that I almost didn't recognise her as the same woman who has sat in this room every Thursday for the past six weeks. She appeared to have little sympathy for her husband's loss, which makes me wonder how she got on with her mother-in-law. It's a relationship that can often be strained, yet regardless of how bad it might have been, her response seemed unnaturally insensitive.

Is she really that cold, or is she attempting to be the stronger of the two in order to support him during this time of grieving?

'She never seemed affected by Mum's death,' he continues. 'Not in the way I was.'

I take a seat. 'No matter how close you might be to them, losing an in-law isn't the same as losing a parent of your own, not if you had a good relationship with your mother.'

He looks at me, his eyes still glazed. 'No,' he says, with a shake of his head. 'Of course not.' He sighs. 'I'm sorry, I shouldn't be saying all this to you, not after what you've been through. She told me,' he adds. 'About your husband. I'm sorry.'

I have made no secret of my loss: there is a tribute to my late husband on my website. I am proud of our marriage; I am proud of all the things we achieved during our twenty-seven years together, even those things we overcame before our wedding vows were recited. Experience is the best qualification I have in offering advice to others.

'I miss her so much. Sometimes it catches me by surprise, this feeling of emptiness – it just comes from nowhere.'

And when it does, it knocks you sideways, I think. Another feeling I am all too familiar with. It has been almost three years since Sean passed away, and though people rely on the cliché of time being a great healer, I understand now that those words are trotted out to offer a sense of hope in a situation where there would otherwise be nothing but darkness. My grief hasn't faded; it has merely morphed into an ever-changing part of myself, something that will age and alter with me, that will stay with me and die only when I do.

'This frustration you say Lydia feels towards your grief,' I say, avoiding any further focus on my own personal life. 'Do you think it might be frustration with herself in some way? Perhaps she wants to help you but is unable to do so because she hasn't been in your situation.'

Josh smiles. It is a smile I haven't seen from him before; not his usual sarcastic, nonchalant sneer, but a real smile that changes his face, softening its hard edges. He holds the look for a moment more than is comfortable. 'How do you always do that?'

'Do what?'

'Try to see the best in people.'

I wonder if he is mocking me. We both know this is far from true – life has made me cynical in so many respects, and he is clearly aware what I think of him. He demonstrates an array of narcissistic tendencies: a lack of remorse or acceptance of any blame, an inflated sense of his own importance, and now, a charm that might easily sway me if it wasn't for my experience and knowledge of men such as him. I have been accused in the past of being sexist, which is entirely untrue. It is a proven fact that a great majority of narcissists and sociopaths are men; it is also a fact that the victims of these men's personality traits are generally the women in their lives.

And yet where his mother is concerned, Josh shows a capacity for love that doesn't fit the outlined characteristics of a true sociopath. Speaking about her now, he seems so different to the man who has sat in this room while his wife has been present. And yet there are others who have managed to disguise themselves behind similar shows of feigned sensitivity. In his case, is it faked? I'm not so sure.

'You have to try to find good in this world where you can,' I tell him, attempting to make the statement sound as casual as I can. 'It would be a pretty depressing place otherwise.'

'I find that difficult a lot of the time.' He stretches out a long leg and turns his body towards me. 'She doesn't understand me. She thinks she does, but she doesn't know me that well, not really. Not like I know her. I feel ... I don't know. I want to be able to talk to her about things, about Mum, but she just shuts off the subjects she doesn't want to discuss.'

'Have you considered the grief counselling I suggested? I mean, properly thought about it? I mentioned counselling to Lydia too, and I know it might not seem that appealing an option, but it could help. You should try it.'

'Did it help you?'

The question is unexpected, though I try not to appear shocked by it. I'm sure others have wanted to ask it, but no one has ever thought to just come out with it before. 'I didn't go,' I tell him.

'How come?' He raises a hand as soon as the question is asked. 'I'm sorry, it's none of my business. I shouldn't have asked that.'

'I can give you a couple of numbers if you'd like them,' I say, keen to brush past the awkwardness that has settled over the room and move the focus of the conversation away from my own history. The irony is that I never went to counselling because I never believed it could help me, but if I say this to a client, then I am inadvertently suggesting that there is nothing to be gained from the time they spend with me.

I go to the sideboard and take a couple of business cards from the top drawer. There are some there that have been given to me by colleagues, and others that were offered to me after I lost Sean, which I then did nothing with. *Lost.* It has always seemed a strange word to use to describe a death. It suggests a carelessness and, in a sense, a kind of blame, as though had you been more careful, the loss might not have been incurred at all.

'Do you enjoy your job?' he asks as I hand him the cards.

'Of course,' I tell him, confident that this, at least, is something I am able to answer honestly.

'Why? I mean, I don't want to be rude, but listening to other people's problems all day sounds like my worst nightmare.'

'Really?' I say, sitting back down. 'And yet a lot of your work must involve much the same, mustn't it?'

He says nothing for a moment, contemplating the similarities between what we do. 'I suppose so. We've probably got more in common than we realise. We both try to help people. We both try to fix things.'

I feel Josh's eyes rest upon my face, and his attention stays with me for longer than is appropriate. It makes me feel uncomfortable in a way I'm not quite able to describe. Whatever it is, it's enough to persuade me that it's time for him to leave.

'Do you think you've identified what needs to be fixed with me and Lydia?'

'I don't think it's as simple as that,' I admit. 'People's problems are rarely caused by a single factor.'

'Really? In my experience, they often are.'

I say nothing to this. Our careers can only be compared to a certain extent, and treating a physical injury is a different process to that of trying to heal a psychological wound.

'Aren't you going to ask us about our childhoods?' he says, when I fail to reply to his comment. 'That's what you're supposed to do, isn't it – listen to our problems and then ascribe all our issues to a single incident that took place way back when?'

'That only happens in films.'

He is different with Lydia not in the room, less angry, the hard edges of his personality softened somehow. He sits upright on the sofa, no longer like a teenage boy who has returned from a hard day of not listening to anything at school, and my confusion about who this man really is continues to escalate. He is a myriad of contradictions: aggressive yet gentle, vulnerable yet suspicious, arrogant and yet somehow strangely naïve. Despite all these things, I believe in what Lydia has shown me of her husband. I believe in what he has shown me of himself. I remember that I need to keep my guard up with this man.

'And I'm not a psychiatrist,' I add.

'What did you study?'

'Psychotherapy – but Josh, these sessions aren't about me, and this isn't a session.' I glance at the clock for the sake of continuing the pretence that we are to be interrupted at any moment. 'My clients will be here soon. Why have you come here today?'

'Honestly?' he says, sitting forward. 'I don't know. I just ... You're not what I was expecting, that's all.' He looks at me for too long, his eyes glassy and distant. I dread another onslaught of tears, but thankfully for us both, they don't come. 'Can I ask you something?'

I nod, knowing that whatever he asks, I'm not obliged to offer an answer.

'Do you ever have strange thoughts? Inappropriate thoughts?'

'This isn't about me,' I repeat, thrown by the unexpected nature of the question. His words intensify the unease that crept up on me moments earlier. Just what is he trying to get at? I am unnerved by the question, suspicious of his intention. He leans forward, his elbows resting on his knees, and looks at me so intently that I suspect his coming here today is an attempt to unsettle me in some way. Ten minutes ago, I could handle him and anything he wanted to say to me. Now, I'm not so sure.

'I get these thoughts,' he says, jabbing a finger at the side of his head. 'They sort of come out of nowhere. I'll be doing something normal, driving or whatever, and they just arrive, whether I want them to or not.'

'What sort of thoughts?' I ask. Curiosity gets the better of me. It is starting to feel as thought Josh wants to confide in me, as though he is building up to some sort of confession. Whatever he has done, I'm not sure I want to be the one who has to hear about it. Yet if it helps me to help Lydia in some way, I know that I must listen.

'Like I said ... inappropriate.'

That could mean any number of things, I think. He could be referring to something violent, or to thoughts of a sexual nature. Things I don't want to be forced to consider sweep through my mind like a film reel, flashing image after vivid image into my brain. A teenage girl on a hospital bed. Him, there, just out of focus.

'Everyone has inappropriate thoughts,' I tell him.

'Do they?'

'Whatever you can think up, someone else has thought it. I wouldn't worry about it too much.' I glance at the clock, making it obvious that I'm doing so. He knows I am trying to get rid of him. The more I attempt not to think about that girl, the more she is here with me. I have never seen her, I have no idea who she is, yet I am able to picture her as though she is a part of my own family, as though I could reach out and touch the pale flesh of her bare arm. As though she is me and I am her, our experiences the same.

I swallow down the bitter taste of bile that has risen in the back of my throat.

'But I do worry,' Josh says, sitting back. 'I worry about it a lot.' He places his hands behind his head and rests against the back of the sofa in a way that suggests he isn't going anywhere. I feel a shiver snake through me, starting at the base of my spine and creeping up and around into my chest.

'I've read up on it a bit. Intrusive thoughts, they're called. You've probably got something about it up there.' He gestures to the bookshelf. 'They tend to be about the same sort of thing a lot of the time, though sometimes they throw something random at me. I used to analyse them a lot, before I found out what they were. I used to think there was something wrong with me.'

I listen, but say nothing. I know what he's talking about, and with anyone else I might sympathise. Where Josh is concerned, however, I can't help but think that all this is leading somewhere, some attempt at justification for how he has behaved in this room and for the way he has treated his wife, because I am sure that thus far I have only been exposed to a fraction of what might take place behind the closed doors of their home.

'These thoughts,' he continues. 'I've had them in this room, while I've been here with you.'

I feel a pulse building behind my ear, dull at first but rapidly stronger.

'You must analyse your own thoughts a lot,' he says.

'I try not to.'

'Doctors diagnose their own symptoms. It's unavoidable. It must be the same for you, to an extent.'

The more he speaks, the more uncomfortable I feel. I shift in my seat and look at the clock again, trying to think how I can get him out of here. I need him to leave, but I know I must be careful about it. I have seen evidence of his temper, and if I push him too far, I will lose any chance to help Lydia.

'Can I ask you something?' he says, still watching me intently. 'What do you think of me and Lydia?'

'What do you mean?'

'Well, just that. Do you think we can make it work?'

'If you want the relationship to work, then yes, I think you can.'

'It's that easy?'

'If you'd like it to be.'

He studies me carefully, his grey eyes casting a steely chill upon my face. 'Have you ever told anyone they'd be better off divorced? I mean, you must have seen all sorts of relationships over the years. There must have been times when you've thought people would be better off apart.'

The headache I had this morning surges back to the forefront of my brain, making me dizzy for a moment. I feel cold, then hot, then cold again, sick with the fluctuating temperature and with memories I would love to bury but am too weak to carry to their final resting place. I would reach for a drink, but today there is no tea tray on the table. 'Once,' I say, hearing a ringing noise start to whistle in my ears.

'It must have been a bad relationship for you to advise divorce. I'd imagine it was extreme circumstances.'

'It was,' I say, keen to end the conversation and get him out of here.

'How bad?'

'It wouldn't be professional for me to talk to you about other clients.'

He smiles and shakes his head. 'Of course not. I'm sorry.' Then he gives me a look I'm not quite able to read. 'And what about us?' he says.

'Us?'

He holds my gaze until I feel his eyes burning my face. A reaction skates across my skin that I know is ridiculous, and I am immediately ashamed of it. What the hell was that? Here he is, talking to me about inappropriate thoughts, and I respond with the notion that maybe he is flirting with me. And for the briefest moment – so barely there that I might convince myself it didn't happen – I welcomed the attention.

I berate myself for my naïve and inappropriate thoughts. I am fifty-six; he is almost young enough to be my son. I think again about the allegation made against him. Was there any truth in what that girl said about him? He wouldn't be the first person to get away with it.

'Me and Lydia,' he says, smiling as though he has read my misunderstanding; as though his meaning wasn't purposefully vague in order to unnerve me. 'Do you think we should get a divorce? I mean, I know you said you think we can make it work, but I suppose you're compelled to say that.'

'Do you love her?' I ask, trying to shake myself from the awkwardness that is still gripping my body.

He hesitates. 'In my own way, yes.'

I wonder what that means, although I'm not sufficiently curious to keep him here any longer than he already has been. 'It's your marriage,' I say, trying to make the words not sound flippant. 'Your way is the only way that matters. If there's still love there, you can make it work.'

I stand breezily and smile, as though our encounter has been anything but strained. 'Keep the grief counselling in mind.'

Josh hasn't moved from the sofa. He is still sitting there, still giving me that look I find impossible to read.

'She's going to lie to you.'

I feel my body tense, but I can't explain why. I have no idea what he is referring to; all I know is that I want to get as far away from this man as possible. I have made a huge mistake letting him in here. I need to get him out of my house. I hear Sean's voice, louder now than ever, and I wish I could call him in. I just wish he was here.

'Why do you say that?'

'Because I know her.'

He stands and closes the space between us. I find myself flinching at his proximity and hope my reaction isn't visible. If it is, I have only empowered him further. My hand slips into my pocket as I reach for my phone. I am disgusted by the thought that crossed my mind just minutes ago, angry with myself for being so vain. Have I become that sad, that lonely, that I could entertain the notion of attention from this man?

'Lydia tells lies,' he says. He speaks calmly, with a matter-of-fact tone, as though this should already be obvious to me. 'It's what she does. She can be incredibly convincing.'

Now I realise what his visit today is all about. He is worried about my forthcoming one-to-one session with Lydia; about what his wife might tell me about the marriage and about him once she is free of his watchful eye scrutinising her every movement. Just what does he fear she might tell me? The truth, I presume. All of it.

He has come here with the intention of intimidating me, and I am allowing him to do so.

Josh has played a role for me today, crying when he needed me to see a vulnerability; smiling when he needed me to see another side to the man who has spent these past weeks dismissing his wife and me with his narcissism and his arrogance. He has tricked his way into my home, his words designed to make me listen and to make me believe that he is not what I have decided upon, because I suspect he knows that my opinion of him has never been set in stone. He is one thing and then another. He is this, and then he is that. He is more than capable of sending an intimidating email.

I remember how he accused his wife of being controlling, and of always wanting him to see things the way she sees them. When I asked him for an example of this, he avoided giving me an answer, instead turning the conversation towards what had happened between them at the restaurant. The opposite of what he claims is more than likely to be the truth. It isn't Lydia who wants to be agreed with about everything. Josh wants things his way, on his terms, and he is prepared to use intimidation to get it. He is the one who seeks control, and he is doing it now, here with me.

'Sometimes people see things in different ways,' I say, keen to gloss over his comment and put an end to this meeting. 'We've discussed this before. Her version of events may be at odds with yours.'

He shakes his head. 'There can only be one truth, Karen,' he says, reaching out a hand and touching my arm. 'Not everyone might like it, but there can only be one.'

I pull away from him, burned by his touch. An image flits into my head once again, vivid and unwelcome: a teenage girl in a consultant's room, sitting on the edge of a hospital bed that has been covered in paper towel drawn from a roll at the end. She is half dressed, the details of her body blurred, but her face is as clear as though I have known her. I don't see him at first, but then he is there: a shadow in the corner that waits just by the curtain and shifts into focus as the picture grows clearer. His face is one I have tried to erase from my memory.

'I'll see you next week,' I say, hoping Josh will finally take his cue to leave. This time, thankfully, he does. I follow him to the front door and close it behind him, turning and resting my back against the frosted glass panel. Things I don't want to think about flood my brain: the way he looked at me, the way he touched my arm, that question that threw up a hundred memories I don't want to have to be exposed to again.

Another voice fills my head, taunting me with its echoes.

What are you going to do about it?

The past stands in the corner, an intruder that throws its shadow across me, suffocating me, reminding me that I will never be free from what happened. I will never escape what I did.

I am seeing Lydia alone tomorrow and I know I must follow my commitment through and meet with her as arranged. After that, I don't know where I go from here. I thought I could do this, but now I realise it is all too soon. I should have listened to the well-intentioned advice of those who suggested I not return to work so quickly after Sean's death. I was reminded that from a financial point of view I didn't need to return to work at all, but what would I have filled my time with then? My clients need me. I need them equally.

And yet it occurs to me sometimes that perhaps I am lying to myself, that I have been doing so for the three years since Sean died. Some days I feel as though I am merely going through the motions, acting out this role I am supposed to play, never actually achieving anything constructive for the couples I work with. Am I really any help to anyone? How can I help anyone else when I am useless to myself?

Glancing up the staircase, I follow the trail of photographs that document the holidays Sean and I shared together. I still can't bring myself to put his face among them, to have to walk past him and say goodnight every evening when I go up to bed alone. If he was here now, what would he advise me to do? I know what he would say, but there is a part of me that will refuse to acknowledge what can be heard so loudly.

Do what makes you happy, he always used to remind me, but I can't listen to that advice any more. All the happiness I have known in my adult life came from him; without him, I don't know what I'll do with whatever number of years I have left. I thought I served a purpose in helping other people, but every time I go back there – each time my mind returns me to that time and place – I am reminded that some couples can't be saved. And now I wonder if Josh and Lydia are one of those couples.

When I take out my mobile phone, there is an email waiting for me. I see the address of the sender, violetsky@gmail.com, and my heart feels heavy in my chest, dragged down by a weight that I am always carrying but that has felt increasingly burdensome during these past few weeks. Whatever is behind the unopened message, it means that the first one I received was no mistake. It was intended for me, as this is. Someone wants to remind me of what I did, though if they realised how much my thoughts are plagued by the memories, they would understand that there is no need to torture me with it. I have done that to myself enough already.

Josh didn't send this message; he can't have. He was here, with me, when it was sent.

I open the email.

It's time you paid for what you did.

With fumbling fingers and a pounding heart that threatens to burst from my chest, I call Sienna's number. Though I know she can do nothing to help me – that she can't provide answers to the questions that furiously circle my brain – sometimes just hearing her voice is enough. Listening to her speak makes me feel closer to Sean somehow, transporting me back to a time and place where I felt safe. I need someone to reassure me in the way he used to, though I know there is no one capable of doing so.

'Karen? What's happened?'

The concern in Sienna's voice is mingled with the sound of exhausted disorientation, and I feel guilty at calling despite knowing it is nearly midnight in Australia. She knows I would never disturb her at this time of night unless there was something wrong, and this has caused a panic that I already regret inflicting upon her. She knows what has been preying on my mind these past few weeks, and she will realise why I am contacting her now.

'I'm so sorry to call you late, but I didn't know what else to do. God, I shouldn't have rung … It's probably going to sound stupid.'

'What's happened?' she asks again.

'Someone's been sending me messages. Emails.'

There is silence. I hear my statement played back in my brain and even to myself it sounds ridiculous. The issue isn't anything that merits a late-night phone call to the other side of the world – Sienna is more than likely considering the same fact – but it is too late for that, and now I need to explain my reaction to what I have received, if only to justify disturbing her sleep.

'What sort of emails?'

'I had one a few weeks back – it said, "How do you sleep at night, you bitch?" And I've just had another one.'

'Saying what?'

'"It's time you paid for what you did."'

Once again there is silence from the other end of the line. I already know what is going through Sienna's mind. I head upstairs to my office, clutching the phone to my ear.

'Okay,' she says, after a moment. 'Who does it say they're from?'

'There's no name on either of them,' I tell her as I turn on my laptop. 'The address is violetsky@gmail.com.'

'Violet sky?' Sienna repeats. 'Does that mean anything to you?'

'No, nothing.'

'Was your name mentioned in either of them? Are they actually addressed to you?'

'No, my name's not there, but they were sent to my email address.'

'Someone's probably got the wrong address,' she says, her voice soothing as she attempts to calm my concerns. 'It sounds like a prank to me, someone just messing around, that's all. Take no notice. I get so much junk mail – if I had a pound for every email telling me I'm in line for some huge inheritance, I really would be rich.' She laughs, but the sound is brief and is followed by another pause. 'Are you okay, Karen? You sound tired.'

She doesn't need to say it: her meaning is obvious. She thinks I'm overreacting, or that I'm confused; she believes the messages may not be quite as I'm relaying them to her, or perhaps she doubts they exist at all. She knows about the pills I've taken in the past to try to help me sleep; she is aware that a cocktail of alternatives has gone before them. The knowledge doesn't help make my suspicions credible.

'I'm fine,' I snap, realising too late that my tone is unnecessarily abrupt.

I open the internet browser on my laptop and type the words 'violet sky' into the search engine. One click takes me to a long list of search results, which at first glance offers nothing more than links to weather-related sites and Photoshopped images that look too beautiful to possibly be real. They are the type of skies I imagine Sienna to live beneath, and Christopher too, wherever he might be now.

'Even if they were meant for you,' Sienna says, too polite to comment on my irritability, 'what could they refer to? "It's time you paid for what you did." Paid for what? You've not done anything, have you.'

You've not done anything, have you. A statement, not a question. We both know what she's referring to, but it is something we will never agree on. Sienna was just a child – she doesn't know the details of that time. I will never forgive myself for what happened. She can't convince me that it wasn't my fault. No one can.

'Honestly, Karen,' she continues. 'You need to try not to worry yourself with this.'

'That couple I mentioned,' I say, feeling trepidation at giving air to the uncertainties I have experienced since Sienna and I last spoke. 'There's something not right about them.'

'You said you didn't think anyone was in danger.'

'Not at first, I didn't, but now I don't know. There's just something off about them,' I add, realising my description of the situation is a poor one at best.

I click on the second page of internet results for 'violet sky', but I'm wasting my time – there is nothing here of any use to me.

'He's controlling her, I think – she never seems to say everything she wants to say; it's as though she's always holding something back. And the husband is constantly on edge, but not in a normal way, not in the way some people naturally are when they come to me for help. He came here on his own today; he's not long left. He was completely different without his wife here.' I stop myself from telling her I thought he was flirting with me. She really would think I'm starting to lose my mind if I did. 'I want to help them, but I feel as though I'm missing something somewhere.' I pause and take a breath, aware that my words are falling into one another in their desperation to be freed. I know what I want to say, but I realise what Sienna will think of me. 'I can't stop thinking about Christine Blackhurst,' I admit.

She says nothing for a moment, and there is little reassurance in her silence. It feels as though she is preparing how best to advise me that I should take a break. Before this second email, perhaps I might have agreed that that was all I need.

'You don't have to see this couple again,' she tells me. 'If you're not comfortable around them, cancel their remaining sessions.'

'I can't. I don't think she's safe.'

'You think he's violent to her?'

'It looks likely.'

'Has she told you he is?'

'No, not exactly.'

'What do you mean, not exactly?'

'It's like she's trying to tell me something but she can't say it in front of him. I've seen the way she watches him. And she looks at me as though she's pleading for my help. She actually mouthed the words "help me".'

Sienna pauses, and I don't need to be able to see her face to know what her expression is likely to be saying. 'Have you seen any evidence on her? Bruises or anything?'

'No,' I admit.

Sienna pauses again while she considers what I've told her. Her doubt is louder than the silence. 'You think they've been sending you these messages, then?'

Though she may not intend it, her tone is laced with scepticism. I imagine how I might respond if it was me who was listening to these words, and I realise I can't blame her for her reaction regardless of how much it frustrates me.

'No. I mean, I don't know. I don't see why they would. And the husband was here with me when the one I received today was sent, so he can't be involved, can he?'

'Has either of them threatened you in any way?'

I know now that this phone call is a waste of time. She has asked this question knowing what my answer will be. They haven't caused me any harm; they haven't done anything wrong. All I have is a handful of suspicions that lack any concrete justification, and a head filled with insecurities planted there by other people, people who existed long before either Lydia or Josh arrived in my life.

I need to sleep, but most of all, I need to leave the past behind me.

'No, they haven't. I'm sorry I called you,' I say, and though it is meant with one intention, the words leave my mouth with the tone of another.

'You don't need to apologise. I'm always here for you, Karen.'

It is kind of her to say it, but I know the sentiment is delivered through a sense of duty. I am not Sienna's responsibility. My problems are not hers.

'I'm sorry,' I say again. 'I'll speak to you soon.'

Yet again, our conversation ends with a lie. I return to the email inbox on my phone, staring at the words that await me there, as though by looking at them hard enough I will be able to change their form.

It's time you paid for what you did.

When I look back at the screen of my laptop, I am greeted by a deep purple sky that stretches above an endless clifftop. It is idyllic, beautiful. It is far from something that should fill my heart with dread.

I close the emails on my phone and focus my attention on the laptop, returning to the internet browser and typing Josh Green's name into the search engine. I painstakingly trawl the search results on Facebook, trying unsuccessfully to match the name to the face that has sat opposite me these past couple of months. I try Joshua Green, but still there is nothing to be found: no man who even vaguely resembles the one who was here with me just an hour ago. A Google Image search produces the same lack of results, and when I repeat the process with Lydia's name, yet again I find nothing that leads me to her.

Frustration engulfs me and I abandon my search, slamming the lid of my laptop shut. Not everyone has social media profiles, I remind myself, though it seems strange that there is no mention of Josh on any hospital website. I realise I don't know which hospital he is based in, but there should be evidence of him somewhere. I try to steady my racing pulse and the swarm of doubts that fills my head, suffocating the rest of my thoughts. Some people prefer to shun an online presence, wanting to keep their personal lives private. I have always regarded it as a sensible option, though in Josh and Lydia Green's case, there is only one thought that occurs to me, repeating itself until it cannot go ignored.

Perhaps they don't want to be found.

And if not, why not?

EIGHT

LYDIA

Lydia arrives at the house alone, as planned. Karen invites her in in her usual manner, doing everything she can to present herself as the trusting counsellor and the perfect host. She seems different today, but Lydia wonders whether that's just because they are finally alone, free of Josh and all his childish tendencies.

'How are you?' she asks.

Lydia shrugs and offers an attempt at a smile before slipping off her jacket for Karen to hang up on the end of the staircase. 'I don't think he's happy about me coming here today.'

She follows Karen down the hallway and into the consultancy room. Today, without him there, she can look at it properly. She notices for the first time the titles of the books that line the shelves on the far wall, an array of psychology textbooks and guides to relationships interspersed with a few classic novels that she wonders whether Karen has ever read.

'Has he said that?'

'He doesn't need to.'

She takes her usual place on the sofa and waits for Karen to complete her routine of making tea. She checks her handbag for her phone, knowing what she needs to do; knowing that today, without him there, is the only opportunity she will get to show Karen everything the woman needs to see.

'You were in a controlling relationship, weren't you?' she asks.

Karen places the tea tray on the table and avoids eye contact. Her relationship with her first husband is no secret; in fact, she has shared her experiences in what she obviously regards as an effort to help others who have found themselves in similar marriages.

'My first husband, yes.'

'I read some of your articles before we met,' Lydia explains. 'What you went through was terrible.'

Karen says nothing, and a silence descends, making both women uncomfortable.

'It all sounds a bit close to home,' Lydia adds.

Karen looks at her now, waiting for her to offer more. This is her opportunity; she knows she must take it while it is there in front of her.

'What do you think of Josh?' she asks.

'Does it matter what I think?'

'It matters to me. I wonder sometimes if I'm the only person who sees it.'

'Sees what?'

'What he's really like.' She reaches to the floor for her bag and searches inside it. 'I know what he's doing to me,' she says, unlocking her phone. 'I've read up on it. I read your article. That's how I came to find your name.'

She swipes the home screen and taps on the internet icon, opening the page that shows Karen's piece: *10 Signs You Might Be in a Controlling Relationship*. 'Here,' she says, pointing a finger at the screen. 'Number one. "Your partner suggests that you are responsible for their actions and responses",' she reads. 'He does this all the time, Karen. Any time we disagree about anything and he decides to lash out, it's my fault, as though I've taken control of him somehow. You know what he can be like – you've seen his temper for yourself. He'll never accept responsibility for anything – it's always what I've said or done that's made him behave that way.

Number two,' she continues, returning her focus to her phone. '"Your partner conceals apologies." He's a pro at this. He never says he's sorry. Ever. He never thinks he's in the wrong. He'll say things like "Well, I'm sorry you feel that way" or "I'm sorry you've taken it that way." He always somehow manages to turn it back around on me. He apologised to you, but you had to force it from him, remember? When he snapped at you last time, when we were talking about his mother. It's all part of the charm, you see, to keep you on his side, but he's never like that with me. Is that normal?'

Karen is looking at her with pity, and Lydia knows what her answer would be if she felt able to just give it. *No. No, it isn't normal at all.*

'Three,' she continues, when Karen fails to answer her question, 'and I won't go through them all, don't worry – you don't need me to tell you, do you? "Your partner makes you believe that no one else will want you."' She looks at Karen as she clamps her bottom lip between her teeth, fighting back the emergence of tears. 'You don't see it in this room, not what he's really like. I said he's never charming like that with me, but actually he was once, a long time ago, when we first met. Do you know, for the first six months of our relationship he bought me a bunch of roses every Wednesday after our first date. I didn't expect it to continue – it would have cost him a fortune – but after the flowers stopped so did the niceness.'

She pauses, takes a deep breath; tries to organise her thoughts into the order she wants to share her story.

'He became a different person overnight,' she continues. 'He started telling me what I could and couldn't wear, who I could and couldn't meet up with. I had a friend from school, a male friend I'd known for years. He didn't want me to see him, so we lost touch. He asked me how I'd feel if he spent time with another woman, and I saw his point. I thought that maybe now I was married it wasn't right to spend time with another man. But then it was female friends too. He'd make excuses for why I needed to stay at home – there was something being delivered, or a workman coming to do some job or other. If I said anything to challenge him, he'd call me ungrateful; he'd say he was working all the hours to give us a lovely life and I didn't appreciate him.' She stops and sighs. 'I was pregnant by this point. He'd got what he wanted.'

'A child?'

'No. He'd trapped me. That was all he wanted. We got married when I found out I was pregnant – I thought it was the right thing to do. How 1950s is that? All the compliments and surprises, the little gifts he used to leave around for me … that soon came to an end. I was stupid.'

'Love-bombing,' Karen says.

'What?'

'What you've just described. It's referred to as "love-bombing". My first husband did the same to me. A person showers another person with gifts and compliments – usually someone they've identified as vulnerable in some way. That person becomes a target, in a sense. It's all about manipulation and control. And you weren't stupid, Lydia. You're not the first and sadly you won't be the last. You are not to blame for how anyone else behaves.'

'Were you vulnerable?'

'Once,' Karen says.

It is said with such conviction that she wonders whether Karen really believes it, or whether it is simply that she wants others to believe it. How many times has she told this story, relating her experience as a victim?

'But maybe it is me,' she says. She leans forward and puts her phone back into her handbag. 'You've heard what he's like with Lucy. She loves him. He's well respected at work. His friends think the world of him. He isn't like this with anyone else.'

'Why do you think it's you, Lydia?'

'For the reasons I've just given. Everyone else can't be wrong. Maybe he's right – maybe I make him the way he is.'

'Do you think that's possible? Do you have that much control over him?'

'I don't have *any* control, do I? I mean, it feels as though he's controlling me. Maybe he doesn't realise he's doing it. Perhaps it's not controlling at all – perhaps I'm just looking too deeply into things. He's always telling me I'm overly sensitive. Do you think I'm being too sensitive?' Her words pour out into the room. It feels good, this release, like having a valve loosened and the pressure in her brain eased to a level that is slightly more bearable.

'Have you told anyone else about all this?'

'No. I can't.'

'Do the children see the way he treats you?'

She shakes her head. 'He's very clever like that. Whenever there's an argument between us and the children are there to hear it, he manages to make me the guilty party. He usually brings up my drinking. It's only a couple of drinks of an evening. Do you see that as a problem?'

'Do *you* see it as a problem?'

'Please stop answering my questions with questions.' Her words are snapped and brittle in tone. They take both women by surprise. 'I'm sorry,' she says, pushing aside a length of hair that has come loose. 'I don't mean to be rude. I just … I want someone to be honest with me, that's all. Everyone seems to do the same thing you're doing, skirting around the truth, never saying what they really think. I just want someone to help me.'

'You want someone to tell you what to do?'

'There we are, you see. You just did it again.'

Karen sits back, widening the distance between them. 'I don't think it's you, Lydia, okay? Is that what you'd like me to say?'

'Not if it's not true.'

There is a pause. 'I always tell the truth. There's no point to this otherwise.'

Lydia nods and mirrors Karen's posture, sitting back on the sofa, exhaling as her body relaxes. She reaches up and puts her hands behind her head, undoing the knot that holds her hair in place before securing it again. She catches Karen's eye as she sees them for the first time: a smattering of dark bruises patterning the pale flesh beneath her arms, round and neat; perfectly set apart at the distance of fingertips. Josh's fingertips.

She lowers her arms quickly and looks away, waiting for Karen to skirt past what she has just seen; knowing that she won't. She doesn't.

'Did Josh do that to you?'

'It's nothing,' she says, smoothing the short sleeves of her dress as she avoids eye contact with the counsellor.

'You're bruised. It doesn't look like nothing.'

When Lydia doesn't speak, Karen presses her further. 'How did you get them?'

She falters on her answer, allowing her cheeks to turn to flame under the heat of Karen's attention. 'Oh, you know how it is. Play-fighting with the kids, that's all.'

She realises the impact of her choice of phrasing. Karen doesn't know how it is: she doesn't have any children. She might have had them, once, but the opportunity was stolen from her.

'You wanted this hour alone, Lydia,' Karen says, her face softening. 'There was a reason for that.'

'I just want to know what you make of Josh.'

'It doesn't matter what I make of him. What matters is whether you want to stay in your marriage.' Karen looks at Lydia's arm, the intention in her words obvious.

'Do you think I should?'

'I can't answer that for you, Lydia. I can listen and I can advise you. I can't tell you what to do. No one can do that.'

'Josh gets angry, you know that. I just wanted to see you alone to … you know … I think you understand me, don't you? You understand the situation I'm in.'

'I think I understand,' Karen admits.

'Despite everything, I still love him. I think you understand that too, don't you?'

Karen doesn't respond to the question, giving her the answer she needs. They sit in a silence that feels heavy in the room, as uncomfortable as though Josh is there with them once again, his unnerving presence felt even in his absence.

'Explain to me how Josh makes you feel,' Karen says eventually.

'Angry,' she admits. 'He makes me feel like nothing. When I'm around him, I feel as though the colour is drained from everything and there's nothing to look forward to, but when he's not there, I miss him. It's like a need, does that make sense? It's as though he's a part of the air. I can't breathe when he's gone.'

She watches Karen's reactions to her words play out on her face: the curl of her lip at the corner, the tilt of her head, the furrowing of her brow as she tries to comprehend something she obviously has yet to understand.

'He suffocates me,' she continues. 'I feel as though I'm living the wrong life. I could have done so much more.'

'You're still young,' Karen tells her. 'You can do whatever you want.'

'That's not true, though, is it? It's a nice idea, but that's all it is. I'm trapped. By him. By our past.' She stops and smiles, though there is no happiness in the expression. 'I made promises,' she says with a shrug.

'Does the idea of being on your own frighten you?'

She shakes her head. 'Not at all. If anything, it's quite an appealing prospect.' She leans back against the sofa, presses her head against the cushion. 'But I can't do it. I could never do it.'

'Why not?'

She hesitates. 'My vows. Don't they mean anything?'

'Vows are important,' Karen says, 'of course they are. But you're important too, Lydia. And unfortunately, not everyone stands by the vows they make.'

'But if he makes a mistake and I walk away as a result of it, doesn't that make me as bad as him?'

'A mistake?'

She watches as Karen's gaze falls back to her arms, and to the sleeves that cover the bruises she has seen. She knows what she's thinking: they were no mistake.

'Marriage should be fulfilling,' Karen tells her. 'I'm not suggesting it's always easy – that would be unrealistic – but it should make you feel better about yourself, not worse.'

'And when it doesn't?'

'You have to decide what's best for you.'

Lydia leans to the floor and picks up her handbag and jacket, slinging both over her arm. There is nothing more that can be achieved here today.

'I have to make this work,' she says. 'I need to stay for the children. They're the most important thing, aren't they?'

With this, she knows the session is finished. Because after everything else that has happened, she knows that this is the one thing Karen won't be able to argue with.

'You're no less important, Lydia.'

'You're right,' she says, standing. 'I know you're right.'

Karen's face says she doesn't believe Lydia will take action. The counsellor doesn't know her at all.

NINE

KAREN

The day after my one-to-one session with Lydia, I am at the front door saying goodbye to a couple of clients when a delivery van pulls up on the other side of the street. The driver gets out and takes something from the back of the van before crossing the road and heading for my house.

'Karen Fisher?' he asks me, glancing down to double-check the address on his delivery note.

I think I manage to nod, but I find myself unable to form words; my voice is lost somewhere deep within me, my throat constricted at the sight of what he holds out towards me, his arm outstretched as he waits for me to take the bouquet of flowers from his hand. It is a bunch made up of the same flower, dozens of them gathered together and tied in a narrow white ribbon that is stark against the deep purple of the petals. Violets.

My eyes scan the bouquet for a card, but there doesn't appear to be one. 'Is there a note with them? A message?' My voice is shrill and panicked, and the delivery man gives me a strange look. 'I'm just wondering who they're from,' I add, trying to calm the quivering in my voice.

The truth is, I don't need a note. I know who they are from, and yet, of course, I don't.

'Sorry,' he says with a shrug. 'I just do the deliveries. Have a good day,' he adds, already turning to go back to his van.

I look down at the spray of purple flowers in my hand as the pounding in my head builds to a crescendo. When I look up, Lydia is standing in front of me, having approached so quietly that I didn't hear her arrive.

'Can we talk?' she says. 'Please.'

I glance along the pavement, as though half expecting to see Josh, though I know she wouldn't have brought him here with her, not today, not after what happened last night. She called me this morning to find out whether I had any free time to see her this afternoon, and I didn't need to ask whether she meant alone.

I feel the bunch of flowers shake slightly in my hand, their petals trembling as I try to steady myself, and I tell myself that I am overthinking things. There will be an explanation for this. I will call the florist – the name is on a tag at the bottom of the cellophane – and they will be able to tell me who sent the flowers. Taking a deep breath, I try to reassure myself that everything is fine.

'Beautiful flowers,' Lydia says, stepping towards me. 'Is it your birthday?'

I stare at her for a moment too long before answering. 'No.'

Despite already knowing that she would come here today, I feel the same way I did when I saw Josh alone on the street, the same desire to turn and hide clutching at my insides, Sean's voice still resonating in my ear. Before speaking with Lydia yesterday, thoughts of the couple's online absence and the emails that have landed in my inbox consumed my brain, overshadowing anything else I might have been able to focus on. After seeing her, all I could think about was the bruising on her arm. All I could focus on were the things I know her husband has done to her.

Now, in the aftermath of what happened last night, my hesitance at welcoming her into my home is marked with something different, something that feels more personal than I know it should. Though she owes me nothing – not even an explanation – it feels as though Lydia has deceived me.

I go to an art class every Tuesday evening in a church hall not far from where I live. I've been going for a while now, after it was suggested I take up something creative as a form of therapy after Sean died. I was sceptical at first – despite having recommended art and writing as therapy to countless people during my career, I was for some reason adamant that there was nothing either could offer me in my grief – but there were people there I got on well with and it came as a pleasant surprise that painting was something I wasn't disastrous at. What was initially intended to be a trial run of a month or so turned out to be something I enjoyed and decided to try to pursue and hopefully improve at.

For the past year or so the evening has ended with a visit to a nearby pub with the tutor and a few of the other women from the class. We don't stay long – everyone has children or partners to get home to – but that extra hour out delays having to come back to this empty house and the silence that fills it; a silence I listen to in the long hours of each sleepless night, awaiting the arrival of yet another alien morning.

It was the turn of one of the other women to get the drinks in, and I went with her to the bar to help her carry them back to the table. We made small talk about that evening's session and the pieces we'd produced; we had been working on self-portraits for the previous few weeks, our efforts to capture a version of ourselves in oil causing much hilarity when it finally came to sharing the finished products. Both balancing trays laden with glasses, we headed back to the far end of the pub, where our group had found the only vacant table that was left. I was mid sentence when I saw Lydia, my ramblings about a potential title for my unintentionally abstract self-portrait brought to an abrupt stop. The glasses on my tray tinkled against one another as my hands shook, steadying themselves in time to stop me from dropping the drinks. I thought at first that I had mistaken a stranger for her, a woman who looked very much like her but wasn't. She was wearing her hair differently, loose down her back; in the tightly knotted bun in which she usually wears it, I hadn't realised she had so much hair or that it was so thick. She was turned slightly away from me so that she didn't notice me at first, and it gave me enough time to absorb the details of what I was seeing without being caught in the act of gawping.

She was sitting in a corner booth of the pub, her legs pulled up onto the bench on which she was seated. She looked glamorous in a way I hadn't seen her before, her face made up, smoky-eyed, and her body language seemingly carefree. She was wearing a short leather skirt that had risen where she sat, her legs covered in sheer tights that revealed the shapeliness of her thighs. The fingers of her left hand rested on the stem of her wine glass – her engagement ring glittering beneath the soft lighting – and her head was tilted to one side, her hair cascading down her back in heavy waves. Her other arm was looped around the shoulder of a man: a man quite obviously younger than her; a man who was definitely not her husband.

Thankfully, the conversation around my table was in full flow, the other women discussing the denouement of a television show that had been aired the night before. Their detailed analysis of the show's final few moments meant that none of them had noticed I had been distracted, so I was spared the awkwardness of having to find a lie to replace the truth of what had taken my attention from our table.

I watched as Lydia laughed at something the man said, as she leaned towards him and whispered in his ear. Unable to tear my eyes from their corner of the room, I watched as they kissed. It was long and lingering; she pressed her body into his, pushing him against the back of the bench. I felt like an intruder, as though I had entered a moment far too intimate to be played out in the corner of a busy bar, and yet I continued to watch as she pulled away from him, said something else, then turned to see me looking directly at them. Her face changed in an instant as her eyes met mine, and I stood hurriedly, knocking my thigh against the table and sending a wine glass toppling.

'I am so sorry,' I said, scrabbling in my purse for a five-pound note. 'Please,' I added, passing the money to the woman whose drink I'd spilled. 'Get yourself another.'

'Are you okay, Karen?'

I don't know which of the women spoke to me; my hearing was distorted, as though my head had been submerged in water. With the background sounds of the pub muted to a distant hum, a tinny white noise filling my head, I ignored the question and took my coat from the back of my chair, desperate to just be away from the place. Lydia made no attempt to follow me, for which I was grateful. I left the pub alone, welcoming the pinch of cold night air that nipped at my face; glad to be away from the claustrophobic atmosphere inside the building.

There was one thing I felt certain of: when she looked my way and her expression changed, Lydia was already aware that I was there. She knew I had been watching her.

And now here she is, standing at my front door, more than likely ready with explanations and excuses. And here I am, clutching a bunch of violets from an unknown person I know wishes me nothing but ill, and unable to explain quite why I feel so deceived and let down by this woman standing in front of me, a woman I still hardly know. Yesterday, I pitied her. Today, I feel as though she has betrayed me, as though I am the one to whom she has been unfaithful, and I'm not quite able to explain why the betrayal stings me so personally.

I open the front door but offer no invitation to her to enter.

'Karen,' she says, apparently aware that I am unlikely to be the first to break the silence. 'Can I come in?'

'You lied to me.' Even I am surprised by the abruptness of my words. Lydia looks pained, affronted, but these reactions only serve to heighten my frustration. Just what game are she and her husband playing? They appear to be one thing, only to show themselves as something else. I'm not in this job for the money, though I obviously need to earn a living. There are plenty of people prepared to pay for marriage guidance counselling: honest people who admit their flaws and face their problems head on to attempt to overcome them; people I am able to help because they allow me access to do so. But I can't help Lydia while she's lying to me, and I wonder why yesterday's session didn't seem the perfect opportunity to tell me of her affair.

I would have understood, wouldn't I?

Damien presented a classic form of the love-bombing I described to Lydia yesterday, having done everything I described to her and more. I was just a teenager when we met – I had never known my father, and my relationship with my mother was strained at best. Having spent much of my childhood loveless and alone, I quickly became infatuated with this man who lavished time and attention on me, so much so that I would have done anything to please him, even when those things meant sacrificing my own happiness. I was young, I had no other experiences of adult relationships; as such, I was impressionable and naïve enough to believe everything that happened between us was normal.

The change in Damien and in the way he treated me seemed gradual at the time, but in fact it wasn't; he was a different person within a matter of months. And yet I realised much later, too late, that he wasn't different at all. He was who he had always been, and it was I who was changed.

If Lydia had told me that she had sought affection from another man, I would have understood it completely.

'I'm sorry,' she says. 'Really, I'm so sorry. The pub last night …
I never thought I'd see anyone I know in there.'

It strikes me as an odd thing to say: not that she is sorry for
her infidelity, but that she is sorry she has been caught in the act.
It is the sort of comment I might expect from Josh. I don't know
why I am surprised by it, though. She isn't the first person to be
unfaithful to a spouse, and she certainly won't be the last. If what
I saw of her bruised body during our last meeting is anything to
go by, it is perfectly understandable that she has sought comfort
and affection elsewhere.

'I love my husband.'

'Do you?'

*He is physically abusive to you. You are having an affair. These are
not the things that equate to love.*

More things I cannot bring myself to say, though they should
be the only words that need to be spoken. Yesterday, I told Lydia
that I always tell the truth. The ironic thing is, this declaration of
honesty was a lie. I knew I was lying and so did she; if I had told
the truth, I would have spoken it to her yesterday. If I always told
the truth, I would be telling it now, loudly and repeatedly, as many
times as it might require her to hear it.

I think back on what I saw when she was here just yesterday: the
bruises that stained her skin and the fear I witnessed in her eyes when
she spoke of what her marriage is like behind the closed doors of the
family home. I think of Josh and what happened when he turned up
here unexpectedly. Can I blame her for her infidelity? Isn't it natural
that a woman in her situation, abused and mistreated by the one
person she believed would care for her no matter what, might seek
affection and kindness in the arms of another man? It was something
I myself longed for, though I never brought myself to do it.

Not for the first time this week, my brain takes me away from
this house to a place I have imagined so frequently in my recent

dreams. I am twenty-three years old, pregnant but not yet aware of it. It is a hot July day and I am wearing a sundress, lemon yellow and dotted with tiny birds, their outstretched wings taking flight across the swell of stomach that I won't notice for another month or so. I am beautiful in my own way, but I don't recognise it yet: I have never known it and I won't know it for quite some time to come, once the beauty has already begun to fade and is bidding me farewell.

I am sitting at a bus stop; he is on the other side of the street, waiting for someone outside a shop. When he sees me, he waves and crosses the road. The nearer he gets, the harder my heart throbs beneath my dress. For years at school no one noticed him; he was hidden behind unfashionable lengths of dark hair that kept his face concealed, but when he returned from the summer holidays with it chopped back from his eyes, he found himself the sudden focus of half the school's female population.

We speak for a while – his lift is late – and when he asks me if I would like to meet up for a drink sometime, I hesitate. 'Yes' is on my lips, with all the false optimism of the summer sun that heats my back, but I know I can't bring myself to say it. It is too late, I am with someone else – I have married young, encouraged by my mother and prompted by the expectations of my class and gender – and I am bound to Damien not only on paper but in ways I am unable to describe and won't be able to name until much later, after the education of hindsight. I am playing at being an adult, not yet realising that adult life doesn't need to involve endurance and acceptance.

I remember feeling my face flush as a string of thoughts that I felt a married woman shouldn't have about a man who wasn't her husband flitted through my brain. I wanted to be looked at in the way that other man was looking at me then; I longed to be wanted in the way I could see he wanted me. But I also wished for all these things from Damien, as he had been not that long before, because once the marriage papers were signed and I was legally bound to him, everything was different.

I told the man I was sorry, that it was lovely to see him again but I was married now, and hurried home, feeling dirty in the shadow of my adulterous thoughts. I waited for Damien to change, not realising then that people don't change.

Five months later, lying in that hospital bed with an orchestra of buzzes and bleeps playing out in the ward around me, I wondered how different things might have been if I had only said yes to that drink with the other man. At worst I might have been branded a cheat, but the gossip would have faded once someone else's scandal surfaced. I might have been happy, if not with him then with someone else. My son might have lived.

'Please,' Lydia says, dragging me back to the present. She turns to make sure there is no one close enough to hear us having this conversation on the doorstep. 'Five minutes, that's all.'

I am so frustrated with her, but I try to remind myself that she is not to blame here. No matter what she is guilty of, her actions have been forced by the treatment she has received from her husband. This woman needs me – I saw that yesterday, as I have seen it so many times since she and Josh started coming to me. I can't let another woman fall prey to a man like Damien Hunter. Right now, nothing else matters.

I nod, and she follows me into the house. She looks nothing like she did last night: her hair is scraped back into an untidy bun that sits on the top of her head, and her face is pale, free of any make-up. She looks tired, her eyes red-rimmed and glassy with the need for sleep. She looks once again like the woman who has been coming to this house every week for the past couple of months.

'Does Josh know you're here today?' I ask.

She shakes her head. 'He'd kill me,' she says quietly.

It is just a turn of phrase – a few simple words thrown together carelessly – and yet I wonder whether in Lydia's case they are meant literally. Does she really fear that her husband might be capable of such extreme violence? Does she fear for her life? Does she fear for her children's? Surely if the latter were the case, she would leave him before things escalate.

I reflect on the tragic irony of my thoughts, wishing I had done as much; and I realise that no one can make Lydia leave her husband. She will only do so when she is ready, when she sees for herself just how toxic this marriage is. All I can do is hope that she sees it before it's too late.

'It's not his fault,' she says, as though she is able to read my thoughts. 'So much has happened to him over the years. He can't help himself sometimes. He needs help.'

I see my own face as it once was – the girl I was before my marriage to Damien Hunter. How many times did I make excuses for him, trying to convince myself that he was vulnerable in some way, that he was afflicted by a condition over which he had no control? He'd had a terrible childhood. It wasn't his fault. I told other people the same things that Lydia tells me now, always finding a way to remove blame from him. Despite everything he put me through, Damien managed to make me sympathise. No matter what he did, no matter how much he hurt me, there was always a justification for it, one that would somehow make sense to me and would succeed in blinding me to everything he was and everything he had led me to become.

I stop in the hallway, making it clear without words that I won't be inviting Lydia down to the consultancy room; not yet, anyway. I feel now as though I have been coerced into the problems woven within the Greens' marriage, and it is a feeling of powerlessness I never wanted to experience again. The thought that I need to end their sessions creeps up on me once more, filling me with doubt.

Then, with just one look, Lydia changes everything. Her eyes meet mine, their former glassiness now replaced with tears, and I see so much of myself in her that I know I can't abandon her while she so desperately needs my help.

'That man last night,' she says. 'He doesn't mean anything to me, I swear to you. I love Josh, you've got to believe that. I just … I'd forgotten how it felt to feel normal. I'd forgotten what it felt like to have someone want me, to have someone look at me in a way that isn't just filled with contempt and resentment. But I want those things from Josh, not him. I think you understand me, don't you? Please, Karen …'

Don't beg, I think, and I remember saying the words before, to someone else so many years ago: a woman like me, a woman like Lydia, who needed the advice I wish someone had given me. Christine Blackhurst's face is in front of me, the details of her features as sharp as though she stands before me now, as though I have been transported back to that final session with her.

Don't beg him to change. He won't.

I hear the words as I spoke them then, echoing in my head with all the clarity of a sentence that has only just been uttered and is still ringing in my ears, powerful and alive. The memory provokes a physical response, and I feel sweat pool at the base of my neck, soaking the back of my sweater. I glance at my watch, wondering how long we have before the clients who are due at eleven a.m. arrive. I want to help Lydia, but she needs to leave. I want to protect her, and yet I want to be on my own. I don't know what I want.

'Are you okay?'

She is looking at me with such concern that for the briefest of moments I think I might forget the feeling of sickness that has swelled in my stomach and threatens to make me retch. Yet I don't. I can't forget, not now the memory of that day and of the ones that followed has been planted and is taking root so deeply in my brain.

'I'm sorry,' I say. 'I have clients arriving soon.'

Lydia looks so hurt that I feel guilty for suggesting she isn't wanted here. I am the last person who should make her feel that way, not when she so obviously feels rejected in her own home and by her own husband. Perhaps she is used to everyone shunning her. I can't be another person who does so.

'Come through to the kitchen,' I tell her, knowing that I can't turn away now.

I don't usually invite clients into any part of the house other than the designated consultancy room, but in this instance, I feel Lydia would be better placed away from the memories of everything that has been said within the four walls of the room in which we usually meet. Josh's presence seems to linger there: I have felt his eyes still watching me when I have returned there alone.

'We had a fight,' she tells me.

'A fight?' Not an argument, I think. 'Fight' suggests that things became physical, and I already know how that ends for her.

'He wanted to know what I'd said to you yesterday,' she tells me, ignoring a response to my question; instead leaving me to wonder just how far this fight escalated.

I put the bunch of violets down next to the sink, not knowing what else to do with them. I would like to throw them straight into the bin outside – I imagine taking a pair of scissors to them and snipping the heads from the stems one by one – but I can't do that with Lydia here. It would only lead to questions for which I don't want to have to search for answers.

'And what did you tell him?'

'I told him it was between us, that that was the point of me coming here alone. He just went nuts.'

She falls into silence, reluctant to share with me exactly how 'nuts' Josh became.

And then she does something I'm unprepared for. As she raises her top, I don't know where to look, not at first, but then my eyes can't help but rest upon the bruised flesh that marks her body, blotting the previously pale flesh that lies taut across her stomach. I think she's going to stop, but she doesn't; she crosses her arms and lifts her top over her head, standing in my kitchen exposed in just her bra, allowing me to see the end results of her argument with her husband.

'Oh, Lydia.'

For everything I should be able to say – for all the words I should be able to articulate – this is all I find myself able to expel.

'How can he do this to me?' she asks through silent tears. 'You can't love someone and treat them this way, can you? You can't do this to someone and then act as though nothing has happened.'

You can if you're a narcissist, I think. Increasingly, I believe Josh may fall into this category, despite what happened during their last session here together and the loving son that was presented when he spoke about his mother. Yes, he loved her, but this love could never be enough to negate the way he treats his wife. He is egotistical and selfish and disarmingly charming when it suits. I have wondered just how dangerous he is, given the right – or wrong – circumstances.

Now I need to wonder no longer.

She puts her top back over her head and pulls it down to cover herself, embarrassed now at having exposed so much of herself to me.

'I'm sorry,' she says. 'I didn't mean to make you uncomfortable.'

'You haven't. I'm just very concerned, obviously.'

She recognises the understatement, I hope. I want to take this woman to her children; I want to lead them all to a safe place, somewhere nothing can hurt any of them. I want to see her husband rot in prison for everything he is and everything he is responsible for.

Lydia crosses the kitchen and goes to the sink. 'Do you have a vase?' she asks. 'You should get these in some water.'

'I'll do it later,' I say, not wanting to be reminded of the presence of the violets. The words of those emails are repeating in my head, taunting me with their refusal to leave me. They grow louder with each moment, surging with the force of a migraine.

'I'd like to do it for you,' she persists. 'I've got an eye for flower arranging.'

There is little to arrange – they are all the same – but rather than try to find an excuse that will explain my not wanting the violets on display, I take a vase from the back of the cupboard beneath the sink and pass it to her. I watch as she fills it with water from the tap before setting about the task of removing the cellophane from the flowers.

'You need to get help,' I tell her. 'I know you love Josh and I know you think he can change, but you also know that what he's done to you just isn't right.'

She turns and looks at me with confusion, as though she has forgotten the scene that she was responsible for just moments earlier. 'That's why I'm here. I thought you could help me.'

'I mean specialist help,' I say, shaking my head. 'There's only so much I can do. I know that sounds like a cop-out, and I wish things were different, but you need to be kept safe. There are organisations I can refer you to, and I'll come with you, if you like. You don't have to do this alone.'

When she smiles, I'm not sure how to read it. The expression is neither happy nor sad. It is empty somehow, all the energy drained from her. She turns back to the flowers and begins placing them individually in the water, handling each with care.

'I've lived most of my life alone,' she tells me. 'A little longer won't hurt. Things aren't as bad as they look.'

I say nothing, knowing she doesn't really believe this. I told myself the same once, though deep down I knew different. Things were worse than I could ever put into words, worse than I was ever able to make anyone see.

'He had a difficult childhood. It's not his fault he's the way he is, is it? His mother was an awkward woman, we've talked about that. He finds it hard to get close to people, but beneath it all he's a good man.'

I have heard and seen all this before, far more times than is comfortable to accept. Her words are those of a woman who has lost her sense of what is right and wrong, what is acceptable and what is not. She is a textbook example of someone who has been blindsided by what she believes to be love, and Josh continues to manipulate her with his excuses because her desperate need to be accepted by him makes her vulnerable to his narcissism. Because that's what Josh is, I am certain of that now. Handsome, yes. Charming, when it suits. A narcissist, most definitely. I saw it in our first meeting, in his aloof manner and the way he spoke to his wife. I saw it when he talked about his arrest. Didn't he refer to 'other people's mistakes' when he spoke about the young woman who had accused him of sexual assault? It seemed such a strange choice of phrase at the time, yet in hindsight it says so much about him. He will never believe himself accountable for anything he does, because in Josh's eyes he is never wrong about anything. I remember my reaction to his attention when he was here alone, and I feel a wave of shame wash over me.

'You're hoping he can change, Lydia. You probably think you can change him, am I right? I don't think that's possible. People like him generally can't change.'

It is the most honest I have been with her in all the weeks I have been working with the couple. I am angry, and it must be obvious to her. She has wasted my time and wasted her own. And yet she must love Josh, she must want to save the marriage; there is no other reason for her being here other than that she wants to avoid the outcome of a divorce. And yet I believe that she already knows the truth: that her marriage to Josh is doomed and that now, with her injuries on display between us, there is nothing she can do but walk away. While he refuses to accept any fault, she is fighting to rescue something that cannot be saved. She knows all this; she just wants to hear it from someone else's mouth.

'He's hurt me so much, you know that,' she says, her back to me as she continues her task of flower arranging. 'But despite everything, I still love him. That man you saw me with last night ...' She stops, and I hear her swallow, as though gulping down her guilt and the bitter taste it leaves in her mouth. 'He made me feel the way Josh used to make me feel, but it's not him I want. Please, Karen,' she says, turning to look at me. 'You won't tell him what I've shown you, will you? I want my marriage to work. The kids need him.'

You can't stay with a violent man for the sake of your children. You may think that by holding the family together you are doing the right thing, but what are you teaching them about marriage if they see you staying with a man who treats you so badly and makes you feel the way your husband clearly does? Show your children courage and strength. Show them you are worth more than this. They may not thank you for it now, but they will realise in time that leaving him was as much for their sakes as it was for your own.

But of course, I don't say any of this. I lied to her when I said I always tell the truth, because the truth is that I can't. The words are all there, lined up in perfect sequence in my head and desperate to escape, but I keep them held back, suppressed by the rules my profession dictates and by an experience that has taught me when it is necessary to say nothing. These words have fallen from my mouth before, the truth has tripped from me so easily; later, it came back to haunt me. I learned from my mistake, maintaining since then a neutral position, merely watching blindly – listening with the ears of a person whose tongue has been severed from her head – as people pour their lives out in front of me, their eyes almost always willing me to pass opinion. They want to be told when something is worth saving. They long to be given permission to leave.

When I chose my profession, I did so in the hope that I would be able to make a difference. Marriage seems to mean less now than it once did: it is easily entered and quickly abandoned; it can be worn and removed with the changes in seasons, an accessory that is soon replaced when it becomes outdated and unfashionable. Usually, in most marriages, there is something worth saving: often all that is required is a trip back in time to retrieve what has been lost, that element of something special that was sufficient to unite two people who might otherwise have passed each other by, and though the path back to the beginning may be longer for some than others, it is usually a journey that is worth taking. Yet I have seen marriages in which there is nothing left to cling to: when the right thing for everyone is to walk away in different directions. I see it, but I can only wish I was able to say it. Instead, I repeat back. I listen, I interpret, I rephrase and I regurgitate. Most of the couples I see seem to realise by the end of their third session that I am nothing more than an automaton, programmed with generic phrases and open-ended questions. Their disappointment is tangible, their frustrations justified.

'Why have you shown me your bruises, Lydia? If you don't want him to know about it, and if you want to stay in your marriage, why have you chosen to let me see what he's done to you? There must be a reason for it.'

She presses the heels of her hands to her eyes, closing them for a moment. 'I just want to make it stop,' she says.

I see my own face as it once was – the girl I was before my first marriage – and I am dragged back across the decades, forced yet again to revisit the past. I am back in that hospital room, as I have been so many times in my head and in my sleep since that day: the bleeping of monitors, the white noise of the nurses' voices; the brain-splitting silence that followed, and that continued when I was back home, ringing with a continuity I believed would be permanent. Sometimes, no matter how hard I try to escape it, I have no choice but to return there.

I am so sorry, Mrs Hunter.

I was young, I had no independence; I had relied on Damien for everything, having embedded myself in the trap he had carefully set for me. I had been scared by the two lines that had emerged on that stick, filled with self-doubt and with the fear that I wasn't ready; that I would never be ready, and that I would never be good enough. The weight of imminent responsibility threatened to overwhelm me. After it, there came the other emotions: the panic, the excitement, the anxiety, the anticipation; the swell of love that bloomed in my chest and grew with the curve of my stomach.

There's nothing more we can do now.

In that moment, I hated the nurse more than I hated anyone: more than I hated Damien for what he had done to us; more than I hated myself for having stayed. My anger towards her remained with me for the duration of my hospital stay, until I was sent back home to four walls soaked in the memory of a night that had only recently passed. In the silence, I heard the echoes of his anger played on repeat: the slammed doors, the expletives spat through gritted teeth, the thud of his boot as it made contact with my swollen stomach. I felt the emptiness that had engulfed me when I knew something was very wrong, as though time had stopped and I was trapped in that moment, destined to stay there for ever no matter where my life might later take me. Being angry with the nurse meant ignoring the reality that the man who had ruined everything and was to blame for all my suffering was the very person I had chosen and welcomed into my life.

The hate I carried stayed with me and grew like a cancer, infecting the handful of relationships I still had that had existed beyond the man I had married. Eventually, even those few remaining friend-ships – if I can be generous enough to describe them as such – were lost to the person I had become; a person I didn't recognise and didn't want to accept was really me. It was only years later, when I was finally able to start again – all of me, like a kind of rebirth – that I was able to form relationships, and it was not long after this that I met Sean.

'It won't stop,' I tell Lydia. 'Not unless you end it.'

I watch her as she places the final flower in the vase and tilts it to rest in the position of her choosing. She tips her head to one side as she assesses her creation.

'There,' she says, stepping back to admire her handiwork, ignoring my last statement as though she has somehow been unable to hear me speak. She picks up the vase before turning and handing it to me. 'Where are you going to put them? I don't think they like direct sunlight.'

I take the vase and look at Lydia, urging her to meet my eye. I glance at the long sleeves she wears to cover the marks I know lie under them. A smattering of bruises along her arm, ribs that have been used as a punchbag, but what other injuries is Lydia Green concealing beneath her clothing, and just how deeply do her psychological wounds run? How long will it be before her husband's violence extends itself to their children?

It wasn't my fault, he will say. *This is what you make me do.*

And now I know I can't be silenced by the past. No matter what my previous mistakes might be, I can't allow this woman to expose herself to a danger that might prove to have been avoidable if only a third party had stepped in and spoken up. I need to be the voice she doesn't have; I need to say the things I wish someone had given voice to for me all those years ago, before it was too late. I can't allow her to become another Christine Blackhurst, and so I utter the words I never thought I would hear myself say again, speaking them because I know they need to be heard, and as much as I wish there was someone else to say them, in this moment I am all she has.

'You need to leave him.'

For a moment, there is nothing. No reaction from her, as I might have expected: no silent tears of reluctant acceptance, no nod of acknowledgement; just an expression of detachment that is almost strong enough to suggest she hasn't heard me. She stares at me and through me, as though she is seeing something else. I put the vase on the breakfast bar behind me, hating the weight of it in my hands.

'What about the kids?' she says finally.

'They'll understand,' I tell her. 'Maybe not straight away, but eventually they'll come to know how their father has treated you and they'll understand that you made the right choice for all of you.'

When I reach out to her, touching my fingertips to her arm in a gesture of solidarity, she looks at my hand as though she doesn't know how to respond. We are two women who have so much in common, yet we couldn't be further apart.

'It will ruin their lives,' she tells me.

There is a silence in which she watches me, waiting for my response. If she thinks I haven't considered the children in all this, she couldn't be further from the truth.

'What if it saves their lives?'

Her reaction stamps itself across her features; her top lip curls and her eyes narrow at the suggestion that her husband might ever hurt their children. She shakes her head, adamant that I couldn't be any further from the truth.

'He would never hurt them,' she says.

'How do you know?'

'It won't happen,' she insists. 'He would never lay a finger on either of them.'

'Until he does, and then you'll never forgive yourself for it.'

She grabs her bag, already getting ready to leave. I could let her go – I could let her walk back to her home and to her husband, to a life in which I know she is unsafe – or I could try to stop her returning to a situation that I know will only deteriorate over time. The type of abuse that Lydia has endured only ever gets worse. I have seen it for myself. I have lived it.

'You're wrong,' she snaps.

I reach out a hand again, knowing that I can't touch her this time, but also that if I let her walk away, it will be yet another regret I must then learn to live with. I hold my palm open to her in a gesture of surrender, hoping that what she has seen of me over these past few weeks is enough to convince her that I am on her side. Perhaps I should let her go, but I can't. The fear of 'what if' is much greater than the sickness that roils in my stomach when I think of the past.

'Don't leave like this,' I implore her. 'I know none of what I say is what you want to hear, but I also know that deep down, you know what I've told you is right. Things will only get worse, Lydia – I've seen it too many times. Please,' I say, stepping back as she tries to get past me. 'Just think about what happens next time.'

I don't expect her to stop, but she does. It is as though my words trigger a thought that hasn't previously occurred to her, although at some base level – regardless of how much she may have tried to ignore it – she must have considered the extremes to which her husband's violence might one day extend.

'I love him,' she says. The words sound small and feeble, pathetic in so many ways; so agonisingly simple. Everything should be so easy for her, and yet it couldn't be less so.

I know my words are going to hurt her, but sometimes the cruellest of truths can turn out to be the kindest, and so I speak them anyway, prepared to accept the consequences of their aftermath. 'But he doesn't love you, Lydia. Love wouldn't treat you like this.'

She steps back a few paces and lowers herself onto one of the stools that line the breakfast bar, dropping her bag onto the tiled floor. With her head in her hands and her face hidden from me, she cries. There are a thousand words of comfort I would love to be able to offer her, but I know there is nothing I can say that will ease the weight of the decision she knows she faces.

I wait, letting her empty her sadness until she is ready to speak again.

'You're right,' she says, wiping the cuff of one of her sleeves across her eyes. 'I need to leave him. I'm going to do it.'

She gives a nod as though reasserting her decision, as though reassuring herself that she is capable of what she knows she must do.

'Just tell me what I can do to help you.'

She shakes her head. 'You can't do anything. No one can. I need to do this for myself.'

She stands and puts a hand out to me, which strikes me as curiously formal given the circumstances. I take it in mine, her palm as cold as I felt it on the first morning we met.

'Keep in touch,' I say. 'Let me know you're okay.'

She nods, and I follow her out to the hallway, my heart already filled with dread at the thought of what this woman is about to face. Uncertainty is a particular kind of threat, one that can't be prepared for. Knowing Josh as I feel I now do, I realise there is no way of predicting how he will react to the news of Lydia's leaving.

Maybe she won't tell him, I think. Perhaps she will wait until he's at work to pack her things, get the children and go.

She stops at the front door and turns to me. 'Thank you. For everything.' She leans towards me and puts an arm out. We embrace briefly, but as she pulls away, her hand lingers on my arm, her fingers closing around it. Her fingertips dig into the flesh, and then she pulls away and smiles, the moment over so quickly that I doubt for a second whether it took place at all.

'I'll be in touch,' she says, and then she is gone.

I watch her get into her car and leave. I close the front door and turn back to the house, trying to dispel the ghosts of the past that have gathered in the hallway to greet me now that I am alone again. A face appears in front of me, as vivid and real now as it was all those years ago. I close my eyes, tightening them as I try to will Christine Blackhurst from my consciousness.

When I return to the kitchen, I see Lydia's bag still on the floor where she dropped it. I hurry back to the front door with it, but I am too late: she is already gone. I retrieve my mobile phone from the hallway drawer where I left it this morning, wondering how she got into her car and assuming her keys must have been in her pocket. I search for her number. When I make the call, and Lydia's phone starts to ring, I hear a ringtone coming from the handbag. Of course, I think; her mobile is still in her bag, along with the rest of her things. As I reach inside and retrieve it, I end the call on my mobile, but not before I see the word that fills the lit screen to announce an incoming call from my phone number.

BITCH.

A punch delivered by an invisible force catches me in the stomach, winding me. A sharp intake of breath fills my lungs with air as I press the central button on Lydia's phone, but it is now asking for a passcode, and what I think I saw – what I know I saw – is already gone. With my own phone, I call her number again. The screen in my other hand lights up once more; the word is there again, unmistakable. *BITCH.* My number is not stored in her phone under my name: instead, this five-letter insult stares at me from the screen. Why?

Before I have time to stop myself, I have put both phones down and am scrabbling through her bag, rifling through her belongings: a packet of chewing gum, a petrol receipt, a small leather purse. Fingers shaking, I open the purse and slide an array of cards from one of the compartments. Doubt lurches in my gut as I move aside the top card: a £25 gift voucher for a popular department store. Then I see it, at the bottom of the next card, a membership card for a gym; something so ordinary and everyday yet with the power to send my brain rattling and my balance reeling. The next card is a bank card, and after that, a driver's licence that bears her photograph: not the woman who has come to this house every week for the past couple of months, with her conservative dress sense and her scraped-back hair, but the woman I saw in the pub last night, the glamorous and happy woman who is a far cry from Lydia Green.

I stare at the card in my hand, at the photograph that looks up at me and smiles, mocking me.

The woman who is not Lydia Green.

The woman whose name is Lucy Spencer.

Without thinking about what I am doing, I reach for the vase of flowers and hurl it against the far wall. The glass shatters into pieces as it falls upon the tiled floor, a scatter of purple petals lying among them.

TEN

JOSH

Karen has called Lucy's mobile several times during the past week, leaving voicemail messages in which she cancels all future sessions with the two of them and makes it clear she wants no further contact from either of them. He knows what the messages mean – she has found out their secret. It is just as Lucy planned it. She has told him everything now: how she left her handbag at the house knowing that curiosity would get the better of Karen; how she went back to collect it, and how when she went through her cards, she found them placed in a different order to that in which she had left them. There is no doubt about it: Karen has seen her identification. She knows that Lydia doesn't exist.

And yet when Lucy turned up at the house to collect her bag, Karen said nothing about what she had seen. She didn't question Lucy or even hint at what she now knew.

He can smell alcohol on Lucy's breath. Things are getting worse for her, though she would never admit it.

They expect Karen not to answer the door, but she does. Her face is set in stone; her lips are pursed as though she has a sour taste in her mouth. She looks unusually dishevelled and is without make-up, her skin mapped with fine lines that are more noticeable now that they are free from their mask of foundation.

'I assume you've picked up my messages.'

'Of course,' Lucy says, and smiles. It is a smile filled with venom, and he sees the contempt returned in Karen's response. 'You've left enough.'

'I don't know what you've been playing at here,' Karen says, her voice faltering on the words, 'and I'm not interested enough to hear an explanation. You need to get off my property before I call the police.'

'I don't think that will be necessary,' Lucy says calmly. 'What exactly are we supposed to have done?'

He knows what it is to be on the receiving end of Lucy's anger; she has a temper that is controlled so effectively that it can seem at times not to exist at all. He knows the passion with which her hatred of Karen fuels her intent, and he realises now the extent of her manipulation. He has allowed her to pull his strings, persuading him that they should be here, though he has known for weeks – has felt since their first visit to Karen's house – that this is all wrong. Until recently, things always seemed to be easier when he allowed Lucy to dictate his life for him. Now he understands the consequences of his attitude.

'Fraud,' Karen says flatly.

Lucy laughs. It is a spiteful, hate-filled sound that rings in his ears, and he feels sorrier for Karen now than he ever has. They have made things so much worse for themselves, and now they have made them so much worse for Karen too. But of course that is exactly what Lucy wants.

They shouldn't be here. This is not her fault.

'You offer a service,' Lucy says, stretching her arms out wide as though delivering a sermon. 'We paid you for that service. I don't see a crime in that.'

'I don't know why you came here,' Karen says, 'but whatever game you've been playing, it's over now. It's cost you a fair bit, this little charade. I hope it was worth it.'

'Every penny,' Lucy replies with a smile.

Karen looks at each of them in turn, her eyes wide with disbelief and an element of panic that she is unable to hide. He sees fear in her eyes, and he remembers what that feels like.

'Come here again and I will call the police,' she says, and she shuts the front door hurriedly, leaving them standing on the path.

'Bitch,' Lucy says, her hands balled into fists at her sides.

'What were you expecting?' he says. 'To be invited in for a cup of tea and a piece of cake? If we'd done things differently, maybe she'd still have spoken to us. We could have got to the truth. This isn't her fault.'

'We know the truth already. What is it with you?' she asks spitefully, her voice dripping with anger. 'Apart from the fact that you fancy her? I know you love an older woman, but she's past it even by your standards.'

'You're being ridiculous.'

He could do it now: slap the silly cow from her feet and leave her humiliated on the pavement, but instead he turns and heads back down the path, desperate to be away from this place and as far as he is able to get from her.

'Don't you dare walk away from me!'

She grabs his arm and her fingertips dig through his jacket, pinching his skin. He swipes her hand away, knowing that if he wanted to, he could hit her to the floor as easily as touch her. He has never done it, though the thought has crossed his mind so many times.

'You've fucked everything up, you know that?'

He laughs. There is only one person who is responsible for doing that, and they both know who that is, despite the fact that she still won't bring herself to admit it.

He loses his balance as he turns to her. 'What's his name?'

'What?' She stares at him indignantly, continuing the charade of innocent victim. 'Oh God, you're not still on about that, are you?'

'I've seen the texts,' he tells her. 'I've seen those photos he sent you. They're disgusting. You're a hypocrite.'

'And you're delusional.'

'So just say it, then,' he challenges. 'Say there's nothing going on.'

'There's nothing going on.' She utters each syllable slowly, holding his eye as she speaks the lie, as though those wide eyes are going to be enough to fool him.

'Tell me the truth. I know you're having an affair. You're a shit liar. You always have been.'

'It's nothing to do with you,' she snaps. 'You know, if you had a life of your own, you wouldn't have to concern yourself so much with mine.'

All this time, he realises, he has been focusing his anger on the wrong woman, hating Karen when it was Lucy he should have loathed.

'Who is he? I'm going to find out anyway, so you might as well just tell me now.'

'It doesn't matter who he is.'

'It might matter to Ross, don't you think? How about we call him now?' he suggests, reaching into his pocket for his mobile phone. 'Let's ask him.'

Lucy snatches the phone from his hand and smashes it on the ground at their feet. Shards of broken plastic bounce across the driveway.

'You stupid bitch!' He stoops to collect the phone; the screen is cracked with all the detail of a spider's web, its face fallen dark. 'You break everything you touch, you know that? You're just like him. You're the destructive one, not Karen.'

Lucy smiles that smile again, tilting her head to one side as she studies him. With her make-up on and the mask back in place, he realises this is who she really is. 'Aww, bless you,' she drawls. 'Someone really does have a little crush, don't they? Or is it more of a mummy fixation?'

'It won't work this time,' he says, shaking his head, refusing to be trapped by the bait she is setting. 'You can't deflect the focus from yourself by trying to make me look stupid. You come here preaching to me about finding out the truth, when all the time you've been putting it about like some cheap whore. Is any of this actually real?'

The slap comes from nowhere, hot and sharp; a cutting sting to the side of his face that leaves his ears ringing with a tinny electrical buzz. He raises a hand to his cheek, his fingertips resting lightly upon the flame that has surged beneath his skin.

She steps back and loses her balance, making him wonder just how much she's had to drink. 'You owe me this.'

'I don't owe you anything,' he snaps, and for the first time in his life he realises this might be true. 'None of this is my fault. I don't think it's Karen's either. And it's not yours, Lucy. We need to let this go.'

But he knows she can't. She has come this far, and though he now doubts everything he thought he knew about her, he knows her well enough to realise that there is only one ending she is intent upon.

'Promise me that this stops now.'

She refuses to meet his eye. 'You wouldn't want me to make a promise I can't keep, would you?' She reaches into her handbag and retrieves her car keys.

'You shouldn't be driving,' he tells her, trying to reason with whatever element of common sense might be remaining.

'Oh, just fuck off.'

With one last look at the house, Lucy turns and walks back out onto the pavement, aiming her keys at the car as she unlocks it. He hears her start the engine and turns the other way, walking away from the house where he knows she will be able to see him in the rear-view mirror. Perhaps he should keep walking, but he knows he can't. She is wrong when she says he owes her. If he is in debt to anyone, it is Karen. He needs to warn her before it's too late.

ELEVEN

KAREN

I have listened to their raised voices from the other side of the door, though I have been unable to hear the words that have been passed between them. My heart pounds painfully behind my ribs, adrenaline and anger making my pulse race. For a while, I feared Josh Green, but now I realise my mistake. Though he is a liar and a fraud; though they are both potentially dangerous in their ability to deceive, I suspect now that it is Lydia – Lucy – I should have feared most.

Outside, their voices fall silent, and I sit on the second step of the staircase contemplating what the hell is going on here. My mobile gripped in my hand, I search my email inbox for the messages I was sent, for that elusive question and the sinister statement that have yet to be explained.

After Lucy left this house for the last time, I called the florist who had delivered the violets here. I knew that data protection would prevent me from getting any details about who had purchased the flowers, though I tried to use the fact that I couldn't thank whoever had had them sent if I didn't know who that person was. I gained only the knowledge that they had been paid for using a PayPal account, which gave me nothing useful to go on. I feel sure that the couple outside my door had those flowers sent to me, but try as I might, I can't seem to make the pieces fit together, and the involvement of either Lucy or Josh still makes no sense to me.

Lucy returned to the house not long after I had spoken to the florist, smiling at me and mocking her own forgetfulness as though none of what had gone before had happened. I bit my tongue, my isolation in this house reminding me that if I was to reveal to this woman what I now knew of her, I had no idea of how she might react.

I have believed Josh to be a narcissist, but now it seems that Lucy is something far more dangerous.

The ringing of the doorbell rouses me from my thoughts. A shadow passes the glass of the front door, but I can't tell if it is him or her.

I ignore the first three rings of the bell. On the fourth – after a finger is pressed to the button with an insistency that refuses to be ignored – I get up and move behind the door, close enough now to make out Josh's silhouette through the frosted-glass panel.

'I've called the police,' I say.

'That's fine,' he says hurriedly. 'I don't blame you; it's what I deserve.'

'You need to leave.'

'I know,' he says, 'and I will. I just … I want to explain. You need to know what's been going on here.'

Just last week I would have agreed with this statement, yet now that Josh – or whoever this man is – is standing on my doorstep once again, there is a part of me that no longer wants to hear the truth. Whatever it might prove to be, it is only likely to hurt me.

And yet it also seems to me that I can't possibly be hurt any more in my life than I already have been.

'I'm sorry,' he mutters. 'This isn't your fault.'

I say nothing, not yet knowing what *this* is. I get the feeling now that whatever truth this man is about to lay bare in front of me, it is likely to be far from the one I might possibly have imagined.

'What's not my fault?' I ask eventually.

'Any of this. We shouldn't have come here, and I'm sorry. I'm sorry I listened to her.'

'Did you send those emails?'

'What emails?'

And though he has told so many lies, I believe this response to be the truth. Lucy sent those emails; Lucy sent the flowers. She was brazen enough to turn up here when she knew that they would be delivered to my door, going as far as to comment on them, to stand in my kitchen and arrange them in a vase while I struggled with just how best I could help this woman escape a violent and destructive marriage.

But apparently, according to her phone – according to her – I am the bitch.

'Who are you, Josh?' I ask. I hear the weariness in my voice. I am physically tired, but more than that, it is the emotional drain of these past couple of months that has exhausted me. I understand why Sienna couldn't take my fears as anything more than paranoia. 'That's not your real name, is it? You two aren't even married – I know Lucy's married to someone else.'

In the two days that have passed since I found out Lydia's real name, I have done what anyone in my position might and checked the internet for Lucy Spencer's social media profiles. It didn't take long to find her. I tried to access the private Facebook account that boasts a profile picture of Lucy stretched across yellow Mediterranean sand; her Instagram page that shows a tipsy Lucy toasting the camera with a glass of champagne. Her life is nothing like the fictional Lydia's, and all this time she has been making a mockery of me. I looked for Josh again too, though I already knew I would find no one of that name matching the face that waits now at the other side of the door. I already knew that he doesn't exist. Whoever this man is, his name isn't Josh Green.

'Open the door and I'll tell you everything, I promise.'

'Anything you want to say to me you can say from out there,' I tell him. 'The police should be here any minute.'

He is probably wondering whether I really have called them, but on this occasion, it is more than just a threat. I know I won't be taken seriously – after all, as Sienna reminded me, this couple have done nothing to physically harm me – but perhaps the presence of the police might deter him from trying to take this any further.

Just what exactly do they want from me? Why would anyone carry out this elaborate a charade?

'You remind me of her,' he says. 'It was the last thing I was expecting.'

'You need to leave,' I tell him, though curiosity gets the better of me. Who do I remind him of? Is he referring to his mother? 'Who are you, Josh?' I ask again.

Through the frosted glass, I see him lean against the door. 'My name is James Blackhurst,' he tells me. 'Lucy is my sister. Christine Blackhurst was our mother.'

TWELVE

LUCY

Karen is in the garden, trying to rectify the effects of a month's worth of wind and rain. The flower beds look sorry for themselves in their dilapidated state, the budding tulips and daffodils pushing up from the wet ground and drooping over in the grey air, giving up their ascent after barely breaking through the soil. The path that leads down to the shed is strewn with soggy April leaves, and she brushes them aside, as Lucy suspects she has done with so much in her life. Bags it up. Throws it out. Forgets it existed.

She doesn't know yet that they are there. Lucy knows that Karen went into her handbag; she left it there for that very purpose. She has orchestrated so much to suit her agenda: the encounter at the pub, where she knew Karen would be that evening; the bruising that she knew Karen would assume had been inflicted by 'Josh'. Karen knows that they are not who they have claimed to be, and it amazes Lucy that she failed to work it out for herself.

And now that she knows who they really are, Lucy would like to know what has been done with the information.

She came here at first with a purpose, wanting the job to be over as quickly as possible, but as the weeks drew on, she found herself immersed in her role and in her new identity, so much so that she came to look forward to their sessions with Karen, testing how far they could stretch their assumed reality until the picture cracked and the truth began to seep through. And not just for

Karen, but for James. She knows that despite everything she has told him – despite everything he has seen for himself – he still doubts the truth of their childhood.

She thinks she might hate him. She thinks she might have always hated him.

She has grown to pity Karen her isolated and pathetic life. In a sense, fate has delivered justice enough: Karen is loveless and alone, which seems suitably fitting for a woman who has caused so much irreparable damage to the lives of others. Yet still it is insufficient. Karen has never been held accountable for her role in the events that ruined Lucy's life; she has never admitted that she was in any way to blame for what happened to her parents. Until she does so, Lucy knows that this will never be over, not for her.

She watches through the kitchen window as Karen bends forward to pull a handful of weeds from the still-wet earth. Gardening gloves protect her fingers, covering the array of rings that adorn them; the wedding ring she wears among them still. Lucy knows all about Sean: who he was, what he did, how he died. She knows about the abuse Karen endured at the hands of her first husband and the way in which it has skewed her view of men. It made everything so easy for her.

Lucy has instructed James to search the cupboards for Karen's beloved tea set. It seems fitting somehow that there should be tea for this last session together, just as there has been for every other. He argued with her in the car on the way over, but he does this every time and she has always known how to get him to do as she wishes. He says he wants this to be over, yet here he is again, doing as he's told. He has always been the same, so easily manipulated; a puppet she can control and get to dance as she pleases. The thing with James is, he is so unsure of everything: his past, his child-hood, himself. She is the only constant presence in his life, and his uncertainty makes him satisfyingly pliable.

Yet Lucy has taken no satisfaction in certain elements of what has been unrolled in front of them within this room over the past couple of months. She thought she could trust her brother, but he is yet another person who has let her down. She knew before coming here that he doubted their father's innocence, but she believed that given time he would come to see sense. Instead, that flicker of doubt has turned into a string of questions she hasn't wanted to give him answers to and an anger that has turned itself upon her. Like Karen, he believes their mother was the victim. The abused wife beaten into silence; the innocent party made submissive under the coercive control of a man who managed to conceal his true self from the rest of the world for the duration of a lifetime. They have played out their parents' marriage in this room, bringing the final act to an ending that they are still unable to agree upon.

James places the tea tray on the kitchen worktop beside her before moving to the kettle. 'We need to tell her the truth. All of it.'

'She already knows.'

'This can't go any further, Lucy. You've got what you wanted.'

She says nothing, keeping her eyes on the window and following Karen's movements in the garden. His statement couldn't be further from the truth: she is still a long way from what she wants. That bitch needs to admit what she's responsible for.

Karen turns on the path and pulls her gloves from her hands. Lucy wonders how long it took her, nearly six weeks earlier, to notice that her keys were missing. She had considered the possibility that the woman might have had the locks changed, but no – after finding the keys down the back of the sideboard in the hallway the following week, she must have put their absence down to her own carelessness, believing them to have been there all along, because at that point, she had no cause to suspect anyone; no reason to believe Lucy and James weren't who they claimed to be.

Lucy has scanned the kitchen several times when passing on her way to the consultancy room over the past couple of months; the door has usually been open wide enough for her to be able to study its glossy surfaces and its high-end finish. When she came here alone and Karen brought her through here, she was able to assess it in greater detail, planning what she knew was to come. Everything here is so white and sparse, so horribly clinical, that it makes her want to splash it with colour to inject some life into the place. Red, she thinks. She would like to see it smeared in blood; to see a little death injected into it.

She brushes past the fridge and reaches for a knife from the block that sits near the sink. She sees a shadow sweep by the window, and presses herself to the wall, waiting for the back door to open and Karen to enter the room. She does so a moment later, tracking a trail of wet leaves and soil onto the white-tiled floor, her gardening gloves still in her hand.

She stops when she sees the two of them, her mouth opening but no sound escaping. With a glance behind her, she realises she has nowhere to go, and that if she steps back outside, then she will be leaving them alone in her home.

'What are you doing here?'

She looks at Lucy as though she still doesn't see it; as though she still doesn't recognise the face that has been sitting opposite her once a week for these past few months. Lucy believes that at some subconscious level Karen must have realised before now who she is. She looks like her mother: everyone always told them so. Strangers in supermarkets would comment on their similarities – the same small nose, the same angular features – and each time a comparison was made, Lucy would cringe inwardly. No girl wants to be told she looks like her mother, no matter how attractive the mother might believe herself to be.

The eyes don't lie. And Karen has looked at her – really looked at her, in a way no one has in a long time. She has believed in her.

She has seen something in Lucy, in Lydia, something she thought she could trust, and she has wanted to protect her. She has been so preoccupied with the idea of protecting Lydia that she has made no efforts to keep herself safe.

'Morning, Karen.'

Everything started with this woman. Lucy doesn't know whose idea it was for her parents to visit a relationship counsellor – her mother's or her father's – but she knows that the brief spell of sessions marked the end of her parents' marriage, which marked the end of everything Lucy and James had known their lives to be. The chain of events that followed the decision to come to this woman took a route that no one could have anticipated, but that doesn't mean there is no one to blame. Karen knows what happened. She knows what she did, yet here she stands, all this time later, in her beautiful home, with her beautiful clothes – her successful career unscathed by what she was responsible for all those years ago – and no one questions what she does. No one doubts who she is.

Lucy knows how it feels to be questioned. She has spent her life justifying her place in this world, pushed from home to home, from carer to carer, and she knows what it is to wear a label. Her teenage years spent trapped in a care system that failed to provide what it claimed in its name gave her resilience if nothing else; she knows what it means to fight for something, and now she fights for what she believes is right, and for what should have been done years ago if only someone else had been man enough to see that justice was delivered.

Karen Fisher took her life away. She is answerable for it.

The counsellor jolts back and steadies herself on the nearest worktop. Lucy wonders which she saw first, her or the knife. She holds the handle tightly in her right fist, the blade tilted at an angle so that it catches the light from the ceiling.

'How did you get in here?'

Karen glances past Lucy and looks at James, who is standing behind her. She must realise that they have already been here a while: beside him on the worktop is the tea set he has taken down from the cupboard next to the fridge. Karen glances at the microwave, where she left her phone plugged into its charger. Lucy has already spotted it, and has removed it so that Karen is unable to get her hands on it. It wouldn't be of much use to her now anyway, not while she's standing here facing someone who has a knife in her hand and the intention to use it should it become necessary. What does Lucy have to lose now? Her relationship with her husband is dead: she realised that long before she started these sessions with James. In an ironic way, marriage counselling has been good for her, despite not attending with the man she is married to.

Her relationship with her brother has assumed a similar status. They had a chance to fix things – he has had an opportunity all these weeks to prove himself worthy of her loyalty – but he has chosen to ruin anything that might have existed between them, and so it stands that all familial bonds are dead and there is nothing left for her to hold on to.

Karen Fisher killed her family. She deserves to pay for what she did.

'I know who you are,' Karen tells her. 'And I know why you're here. What was the point in any of this? It hasn't achieved anything.'

'Actually, you're wrong there. It's been quite enlightening really. For one, it's made me realise I don't love my husband any more. My actual husband, I mean. I'm going to tell him we're getting a divorce.' She studies Karen's face as she speaks, waiting for a reaction to the words; words she knows she has heard before, long before they met. She sees it in the flicker of her eyes, though Karen tries so obviously hard to contain the response. 'What's wrong? Has something I've said touched a nerve? Is that what happened, Karen? Is that what my mother told you too?'

Karen is shaking her head. She must be scared – her attention flits from the knife to Lucy's face and back again – but she is managing to maintain an appearance of control. 'This is madness. I want you to leave my house, both of you.'

'Has the kettle boiled yet, James? I think we could all do with a nice cup of tea. What do you think, Karen?'

Karen's eyes rest on the knife gripped in Lucy's hand. 'I think you need to leave this house before I call the police.'

'What are you going to do that with?' Lucy asks, reaching into her pocket with her free hand. 'This?' She retrieves Karen's mobile and waves it tauntingly before putting it away again. 'Your landline seems to be down, as well,' she adds. 'Shame.'

'Does your husband know you're doing this? Your real husband. Ross, isn't it? Not that hard to find, thanks to the internet. I wonder what he'd make of it all.'

Karen's words exude a confidence that Lucy knows is faked. She almost sounds like her, she thinks, as though she is trying to reflect her own air of authority; as though by doing so she might be able to deter Lucy from what she is doing. But she won't. She can't. No one can.

Karen glances behind her again, as though considering an escape through the back door. Startling her with her swiftness, Lucy steps forward and brushes past her, raising the knife to Karen's eyeline as she closes the back door, locks it, removes the key and puts it in her pocket with the phone.

'I doubt he'd be interested. We live very separate lives.'

'So I saw.'

James's eyes narrow and he looks at Karen questioningly, searching for an explanation for the comment.

'Didn't she tell you?' Karen asks, reading the look. 'I saw her in the pub with another man. They weren't exactly hiding themselves. Pretty blatant, actually.' She turns to direct her words at Lucy. 'It was almost as though you wanted people to notice you, in fact.'

Lucy smiles. That was exactly what she had intended. It wasn't difficult to discover what Karen does in her free time: her life is so boring and structured that any idiot could easily find out where she might be at any given day and time. Clients until 2.30 p.m. on weekdays, food shop on a Friday afternoon, art class on a Tuesday evening. It is all so sadly predictable and so mundanely vanilla. She wonders what Karen gains from the tedium of routine; whether she uses it as way of punishing herself for what she is guilty of.

She doubts it. To feel guilty, Karen would have to acknowledge fault.

She sees what Karen is doing, trying to cause a rift between them that might shift the focus away from herself and her crimes. She is set to fail miserably: the relationship between Lucy and James can't be any more frayed than it already is. The damage was done long ago –over twenty years earlier, in fact, when Karen Fisher tore their family apart.

'You sent those emails, didn't you?' Karen says. 'And the violets, too. A nice touch.'

'Violets?' James repeats.

'Whatever you think I'm guilty of,' Lucy says, brushing off her brother's interruption, 'it's nothing compared with what you did.'

'How did you find me?' Karen asks, ignoring the comment.

Lucy had known the question would arise. In truth, it was far easier than she had anticipated to find out the identity of the elusive marriage guidance counsellor. She had overheard enough conversations – arguments, really – between her parents to know that they had been seeing one; all she'd had to do was find out who it was. After her mother was arrested, she and James had been taken by social workers back to the house to collect some of their belongings. That was when she had found the address book that was kept by the telephone in her parents' room, placing it in her box of things as though it was her own. Once she had the address it was easy to find out what sort of 'counselling' was carried out there; all she had needed to do was find a name. That had come years later, once her resentment had been given time to fester into a full-blooded desire for revenge.

'I've had plenty of time,' is the answer she offers. 'Like you said, the internet makes everything so easy now.'

'What do you want from me?'

Lucy looks casually at the kettle before returning her focus to Karen with a smile. 'How about a nice cup of tea for a start?' She thrusts the knife towards her, silently instructing her to set about her task. 'Once you've done that,' she adds, 'you can give us the truth.'

She jabs the knife in Karen's direction for a second time, prompting her to do as she is told. She watches Karen as she pours water from the kettle into the teapot and places everything on the tray that is set ready for her, a repetition of a ritual she has carried out countless times. Watching the woman, she feels a hatred that is more intense than ever.

Lucy's life as she had known it came to a sudden and violent end over two decades ago, when she was just thirteen. After that, nothing was ever the same again. With no other family to take them in, she and James were moved from home to home, branded with the mark of their shared past; she entered adulthood with nothing and tried to regain some control by marrying into wealth. Ross Spencer is an entrepreneur in the field of pharmaceuticals, a self-made millionaire, and the most boring man she has ever met. She realises now the mistake she made, though had she wanted to acknowledge it, she would have been able to admit it years ago: she doesn't love her husband – she never did – but he offered her a security she had been lacking all those years, since the day a grenade was thrown into her life.

The person who threw the grenade is here now, still looking at her as though incapable of seeing the truth that stands in front of her.

'We're going to do this properly,' Lucy tells her, stepping past her to pick up the tea tray. 'Just as we've been doing all these weeks.' She thrusts the knife towards James; he takes it, though it is obvious to them all that he does so reluctantly. 'Follow me. Let's go through to the consultancy room,' she says, mimicking Karen's voice.

'You don't have to do everything she tells you, James.'

Lucy turns sharply, slopping boiling water from the teapot onto the tray. Her face flushes with anger, her cheeks reddened with objection at Karen's challenge to her authority. 'Yes he does,' she says softly, her voice a contrast to the violence she feels building inside her; a violence that is visible to everyone. 'And so do you. Understand?'

Karen follows now, seeming to finally realise that no matter what power she thinks she has, the knife in James's hand cancels it out.

'You know that I can't give you the truth, don't you, Lucy?' she says as they enter the consultancy room. 'I can tell you what I saw, but only your parents know the truth of what really happened.'

'But they're not here any more, are they?' Lucy says, as though Karen needs reminding of the fact. 'And you're responsible for that.'

And now Karen needs to pay for what she did.

For Lucy, Karen's truth is the only one that remains. What she saw – or what she thinks she saw – was the beginning of the end.

Or perhaps not. Things had started to go wrong when that girl lied to the police and told them her father had touched her. Everyone knew she was a liar, even the police, but her mother had decided to believe the allegation, as though pledging love and loyalty to someone meant nothing and could be as easily torn to pieces as the paper the declaration was signed upon. She had always been against him, always trying to make his life difficult. No wonder her father treated her the way he did.

No wonder that James gives her little other option now than to treat him in much the same way.

'Sit down.'

Karen takes a seat on the sofa to which Lucy gestures. Lucy places the tea tray on the table while James lingers near the window, his concentration split between the carpet at his feet and the clock on the far wall. He is refusing to make eye contact with either woman, as though doing so would be confirmation of whose side he is taking. She was reluctant to bring him here with her today, but this is it: he has one final chance to prove himself.

She remembers how her father looked that night she saw him come home late; the night he was released from the police station after his arrest. She had been in bed – her mother thought she was asleep – but when she heard the front door, she went to the landing and stood at the top of the stairs watching him take off his coat and shoes. He looked so tired, so drawn, and she knew even then that something was very wrong. And then there came the argument. He told her mother he was innocent; as far as Lucy could see, that should have been enough for her. He was her husband. He was their father. He wouldn't have done what that girl had claimed.

She takes the knife from James. 'So let's hear it then,' she says, turning the blade towards Karen.

'I'm not sure what you want me to say, Lucy. What is it you think I've done?'

'You know what you did. Just how do you sleep at night?' She tilts her head to one side, relishing the effect her words have on Karen, the echo of the email she sent. Though her message was short, it took an unexpectedly long time to construct. It had to be precise. It needed to have the right impact. 'You took everything from us,' she adds.

Lucy was aware of everything that had been said about her father, but she knew it was all lies. For months her parents continued to believe she knew nothing about what was going on – as though thirteen was too young to understand what a sexual allegation consisted of, as though her hearing hadn't yet developed to its full adult capacity and she was incapable of comprehending the angry words that were passed in badly hushed tones on the other side of the wall at night – but she knew exactly what was happening. She knew that her mother believed what that girl had said.

Her father was a popular man, successful and well respected. He was a doctor, for goodness' sake: he healed people. He had a reputation that went before him; a reputation that lived on long after he had died. For all the letters she sticks after her name on her website – for all her fancy magazine-cover home interiors and her fine bone china – Karen is nothing in comparison.

'Why violets?' Karen asks.

'It's Lucy's middle name,' James answers for her. He stares at her questioningly, clearly wondering just how much she has done without his knowledge. If she had told him, he would have tried to stop her. He thinks things have gone too far, but for Lucy they haven't gone nearly far enough. She doesn't care what James thinks; she never really has. She isn't answerable to him; that isn't the way their relationship works.

'It's after my grandmother,' Lucy adds. 'Dad used to recite a rhyme that his grandfather had written for her. *Hush little baby, dry your eyes, Daddy's going to sing you a lullaby. Sleep little darling, don't you cry, dream sweet dreams beneath a violet sky*. Pretty, isn't it? He might have recited it to his grandchildren one day, but you killed any chance of that.'

Karen is shaking her head in vehement denial. Lucy hates her with a violence that makes her body shudder. How different her life might have been had it not been for Karen's interference in things that were nothing to do with her. This woman took her own experiences, her life with her first husband, and dumped them at her parents' door, leaving Lucy and James to live with the consequences.

'I did what I thought was best. I am so sorry for what happened, Lucy, sorrier than you'll ever know. I was trying to protect your mother. I was trying to protect you.'

Lucy laughs; a bitter, sharp noise that punctures the silence of the room. 'The only person she needed protecting from was you.'

Lucy knows what she saw. She knows what she heard. She was home earlier than expected that afternoon and her parents were in the kitchen. Her mother had planned to pick her up two hours later; she was supposed to have gone to a friend's house after school, but she had argued with the girl at lunchtime and had decided not to go. James wasn't at home; he went to some geeky games club after school every Thursday and wasn't due to be dropped back for another couple of hours.

The kitchen was a mess, she remembers: dirty dishes piled high on the worktop by the sink and clothes thrown against the closed door of the washing machine. Her father was a man of routine and order and he liked the house to reflect his principles, but during those past few months something had happened to her mother. The woman who usually held everything together – if only for the sake of appearances to the world that lay outside their little corner of suburbia – had been replaced by someone who drank wine at the kitchen table into the early hours of the morning and didn't get up from the bed in the spare room until around midday.

When Lucy arrived home, her mother was sitting at the table, her father standing beside her, a sheet of paper brandished in his hand. Neither of them noticed their daughter standing in the doorway, and when she heard her father's words, she stepped back again, disappearing from their view.

When were you going to tell me about this?

Her mother snatched the paper from his hand, scanning it as though she didn't already know its contents. *I've tried*, she said, not meeting his eye. *I've tried everything, and nothing is ever good enough for you.*

Her father stepped back and folded his arms across his chest. *You can't do this.*

Of course, Lucy can't really know what each of them was doing: she was on the other side of the wall. But she thinks she knows what happened. She thinks there is only one way it could have happened.

I can. I didn't believe it until now, but I can and I'm going to.

A moment of silence followed. Lucy held her breath, as though her parents might be able to hear the rise and fall of her lungs from the other side of the kitchen wall. She was used to these silences. She knew how to fill them with noise from inside her own brain; how to make the bad things fade until they weren't there any more and all she was left with was an empty space in which to start again, like a child with a crayon and a blank sheet of white paper.

This is her doing, isn't it? What have you told her?

Nothing. This is about me, Stuart ... just for once, this is about me.

There was a scraping of metal chair legs upon the tiled floor as her mother stood from the table.

She's twisted your mind against me, do you know that? Everything was fine before we started seeing that woman. I told you to leave it, but you just wouldn't let it go, would you?

I was trying to help you. I stupidly thought I could, but you're beyond that, aren't you? You can't help yourself either. This is who you are.

Her father's voice was calm, as it always was. It was only her mother who raged like a crazy person.

I'll take the children. Is that what you want?

No. You can't.

Lucy heard something else then: something crashing to the floor as it was knocked from a worktop. Later, she saw it was the blue patterned vase her father had bought her mother as an anniversary present, years earlier. It was beyond repair. Something in so many pieces wasn't worth trying to save.

Don't! Get off me!
I won't let you do this!

Lucy's body stiffened at the sounds that followed: the scuffling
of feet along the kitchen floor; the cupboard door that was smashed
shut; the dull thud; the single guttural groan. She waited for what
would come next, but all that filled the hallway was an awful deathly
silence that seemed to last for ever. When she finally moved, she
went into the kitchen with her breath held, not knowing what she
might find; not ready to face what she was unable to bring herself
to imagine.

Her mother had fallen back against the fridge, her chest heaving;
her lungs gulping ragged gasps that punctuated the silence of the
room. Pieces of blue china lay scattered at her feet. Amid them lay
the divorce papers her husband had thrown back at her. Her eyes
were fixed on the other side of the kitchen; Lucy followed their
path to where her father sat slumped against a cupboard, a knife
plunged into his chest, his shirt stained in bursts of red that had
patterned the fabric with a macabre Valentine's bouquet.

Her mother later claimed self-defence, but Lucy knew what
she had heard.

'I'm so sorry, Lucy,' Karen says, as though she knows where
her mind has been; as though she has an idea of what Lucy has
imagined, though she can't possibly know anything of what she
has been through. 'You should have told me who you were. We
could have talked about all this.'

But Lucy knows she's only saying it because there's a knife in her
hand. If she had turned up here months ago and introduced herself
as Lucy Blackhurst, daughter of Stuart and Christine, she can only
imagine what Karen's reaction might have been. She doubts very
much that she would have been invited in for tea.

'He hurt her, didn't he?'

Until now, Lucy has almost forgotten that James is in the room
with them. He is still standing at the window, still holding his head

lowered and staring at the carpet as though if he looks hard enough the floor might give way and he'll find an escape route from this room. Of all the things he might have asked her, Lucy can't believe that this is it. It shouldn't surprise her: he came here with doubts, and over the weeks, Karen has managed to persuade him that she is a trustworthy person, someone who has only their best interests at heart. He has fallen for her charms, yet another of her victims.

Karen nods. 'I know it's not what either of you want to hear, but your father inflicted years of abuse upon your mother. I'm sorry,' she says, raising a defensive hand in Lucy's direction, 'but that's the truth of it. I know it's difficult for you to accept, but she kept so much hidden to protect you. She loved you two more than anything, you must believe that.'

'I don't believe a word you say,' Lucy says slowly. 'You lied to the police and now you're lying to us. My father was a good man.'

'He wasn't, though, was he, Lucy?'

She turns sharply at her brother's words. 'What do you even know about anything?' she snaps. 'You were just a kid; you didn't have a clue what was going on.'

James shakes his head, exasperated. 'I was nine, Lucy. I saw and heard plenty. Remember that time Mum fell down the stairs—'

'When she was pissed, you mean?' Lucy says, cutting him short.

'She didn't fall because she was drunk,' he objects. 'She fell because he pushed her.'

Lucy shakes her head and stares at him defiantly. 'You're wrong.'

'I'm not. And I'm not wrong about his death either. She was defending herself, Lucy.'

She doesn't want to hear the words; they are poison poured in her ear by a man who despite his age is still little more than a boy: a boy who only saw half-truths and used them to construct an incomplete story in his underdeveloped, childish brain. He played a man seven years older than her to meet their parents' age difference, but this element of his performance was always the least convincing. What she said about him all those weeks ago was true: there was always something wrong with him. He wasn't like any other kid she knew; he was withdrawn and secretive and just downright strange. He shut himself off from normal things in the same way their mother had, shunning interaction with other people and existing in his own little world of make-believe. Everyone said he was odd: teachers, medics, friends. Everyone saw what was happening to him, except their mother. No one took him seriously as a child and no one will listen to what he has to say now. Except, perhaps, Karen Fisher.

Lucy knows what happened – she was there. Her parents argued over the divorce papers her mother had applied for after Karen told her she needed to leave her husband. When questioned by police following the death of Stuart Blackhurst, Karen Fisher claimed that Christine had endured years of emotional and psychological abuse at the hands of her husband, admitting that she had advised her client to seek a divorce. Yet no one else had seen any signs of abuse. Christine Blackhurst was a bit of a recluse, they said; she seemed socially awkward, the type of woman who preferred to keep herself to herself. No one knew what a handsome, successful man like Stuart was doing with a woman like that. People had pitied him, being tied down to such a strange and lonely character. She had done a good job in convincing the counsellor she was a victim, but nobody else was going to fall for the lie.

Karen Fisher killed Lucy's parents. She took Lucy's life away. It seems only fair that she should now pay with her own. Lucy's fingers tighten around the handle of the knife. She wonders if this is how Christine felt, moments before she plunged the blade into her father's chest. She had hoped to take everything that was his: his money, his house; his children.

'I know Mum seemed strange at times, not like normal mums, but have you ever asked yourself why that was?' says James.

'Normal mums,' Lucy repeats. 'Exactly. All that drinking in the house, never doing anything or taking us anywhere – that wasn't normal. What about that time at the neighbours' house, when we went over there for a barbecue? And that time in the restaurant, when she flirted with the waiter – that wasn't normal either, was it?'

Lucy glances at Karen, sees the picture falling into place as the conversations of those past weeks form an entirely different meaning. She remembers that night at the restaurant so clearly, the details of it imprinted on her brain as though it was just yesterday. She felt so sorry for her father that night. Her mother had dressed in a way she and James had never seen before, in a skirt that was far too short for a woman of her age and a low-cut top that revealed an embarrassing amount of flesh; Lucy knows that if they had left the house together, her father would never have allowed her to go out dressed like that. It wasn't right: Christine was a woman in her thirties, not some teenage girl trying to impress on a first date. Lucy remembers how embarrassed she was by her mother's drinking, and how the emptier the wine bottle became, the louder her mother's voice grew. She persisted in making snide comments to their father, belittling him at every opportunity. Next to her, James was disappearing inch by inch behind the cover of his comic book. He was only nine at the time. He can't remember things as they really were.

'I don't think any of it was normal, Lucy. It might have seemed that way at the time because that's all we were used to, but now, looking back ... I think it was a cry for help. She wanted people to see what was going on, that there was something wrong.'

Lucy scoffs and shakes her head. 'You don't know what you're talking about. You were too young, but trust me, I remember.'

'You've remembered the parts you want to remember,' he says. 'What about all the times Mum stayed up in her room and he'd make excuses for her, saying she was ill? What kind of mother hides from her children for days on end because of a cold?'

'Exactly … what kind? The kind we were lumbered with. The kind who took our father from us and then killed herself when she realised she wasn't going to get away with it.'

She sees Karen flinch at the mention of Christine's suicide. Though she may have tried for all these years, she can't possibly have forgotten what she was responsible for. James is shaking his head, intent on disagreeing with everything Lucy has told him. He thinks he understands what went on, but she knows he can't possibly comprehend the kind of relationship their parents had. Her father did everything for her mother, gave her everything, and she repaid him with the threat of divorce. She showed her gratitude by threatening to rip his life from under his feet.

'She was hiding her bruises,' James says, his voice rising. 'How can you be so naïve? Why are you so blinded by that man that you refuse to see him for what he really was?'

'How do you know that?' she challenges. 'How do you know there were bruises at all?'

'They were there,' Karen says. 'I saw them.'

'You saw these as well.' Lucy pushes her sleeve up her arm and lets her fingers trace the pale skin on which the bruising has only just begun to fade. It was all so easy; too easy, if anything. Her husband was so excited by the prospect of being allowed anywhere near her naked body that she didn't need to encourage an enthusiasm that had easily gone beyond the boundaries to which they had previously ventured. She needed to add to the damage later, when she was alone; it hurt, but she couldn't possibly hurt any more than she already was. Physical suffering seemed nothing in comparison to the pain that had existed in her head for so many years, and she knew it would all be worth it in the end.

The man she'd been having an affair with for the past six months wasn't too impressed when he saw the evidence of sex with the husband she claimed not to have gone anywhere near in years, but he was hardly able to complain: he was sleeping with a married woman; she was never his exclusively. She would have preferred it to be him who inflicted the bruises, but having to find an excuse to explain that away to her husband was something she simply couldn't be bothered with.

She drops her sleeve, her point made. 'We just see what we want to see, don't we, Karen?'

She knows she has flustered her, making her question everything she thought to be real. If Lucy managed to fool her, then why can't the same be said of Christine?

Karen shakes her head. 'I know what I saw. Not just of your mother, but of your father. I know what he was, Lucy.'

Lucy steps towards her, holding the knife in line with the other woman's throat. How easy it would be, she thinks, to just end it all here, to watch her fall at her feet and know that justice has finally been delivered. But it would be over too quickly, the pain ended too soon. Lucy has suffered for decades. Karen deserves something more.

THIRTEEN

KAREN

I hadn't expected to see either of them again, although I knew as soon as I stepped into the kitchen just how naïve that thought had been. Perhaps I believed that James had been able to convince his sister of the absurdity of their charade, or maybe I assumed that Lucy had grown bored of playing Lydia and would focus her energies elsewhere. Either way, I realise their commitment to this game they have been playing these past couple of months far exceeds my expectations. I wonder now just how far they will take it. How does this all end?

Lucy is standing in front of me, her eyes ablaze with a hatred that manages to exude a stifling heat. I feel her anger scorch my skin as though she has taken a match to my flesh, and a headache pulses between my eyes, blurring my vision and making me dizzy.

Knowing now who he really is, I have searched online for James Blackhurst, but he keeps a low profile, with no social media accounts boasting of his antics. I haven't been able to find out anything about him: where he lives, where he works, whether he has a family of his own. Lucy doesn't have a job; she has no need for one. It appears her wealthy husband funds the lavish life of luxury her social media posts would have everyone believe she lives. And yet I suspect that is all it is: appearance. Nobody truly happy and content with their own life could wish to wreak mayhem on another's in the way that Lucy Spencer seems so intent on doing upon mine.

I have also returned to the articles about Stuart and Christine's deaths, reports I have known for years exist online. In the past I have done everything I can to avoid having to look at and linger over them. I have glanced at them briefly, curiosity always getting the better of me, but I never needed to read them in full: I have always known what happened. Their stories are as integrated with my life as my own.

I hold Lucy's gaze, wanting her to believe that I am not afraid of her. The truth is, this woman terrifies me. I know nothing about her: I have never known her.

'Everything you've told me is a lie.'

She smiles at me, perplexed. 'On the contrary … everything we've told you is the truth. It's just not our truth. That doesn't make it any less real, does it?'

I don't know what more I can say to her. Lucy is fixed on her beliefs and it appears they are unchangeable. Though both she and James are here, I realise their motives over these past couple of months have been entirely different. For Lucy, this has been about revenge. For James, it is about finding the truth; a truth that in his heart I know he already believed before coming here for the first time. He just wanted to have it confirmed.

I called the police. Realising what had been happening here over these past couple of months, and knowing that one of them – presumably Lucy – was responsible for the emails I'd been sent, I called and spoke to an officer who couldn't have sounded less interested in what I had to tell her. She asked me whether either of them had harmed me or threatened me harm. Not yet, I told her, but I couldn't be sure whether they intended to. I couldn't be sure of anything. I heard her sigh at the other end of the phone, with no attempt made to disguise her lack of interest. After explaining who James and Lucy are and how they are connected to me, the officer's attitude was unchanging. Neither of them has committed a crime, she told me. I disagreed. I argued that it was fraudulent behaviour, that it was intimidating and threatening, but I knew I was getting nowhere. She told me there was nothing they were able to do unless the situation escalated.

And now they are here, with Lucy right in front of me, a kitchen knife clutched in her fist. Has the situation escalated enough now?

'So tell me,' she says, stepping away from me and sitting at the opposite end of the sofa, resting the hand that holds the knife on her knee. 'What was my father like then? You seem to have known him so well – far better than his own children ever did.'

I know that the rational, sensible thing to do here would be to give an account of Stuart Blackhurst as the man she believes herself to have known: the long-suffering husband and loving father; the man wrongly accused of a crime for which he was later found not guilty. Perhaps there is no one left to hurt in telling the lie, but despite this, I know I can't do it. Stuart Blackhurst assaulted that girl, of that I have always been convinced. She would be in her late thirties now, not much older than Lucy is – not much older than Christine was when she came to me for help – and if I speak these words – if I tell this lie that has already been uttered far too many times – I make a mockery of his victim, yet another person to fail her in denying what that man was.

'Your father had a narcissistic personality disorder.'

Her eyes narrow at the words; on her knee, her hand tightens its grip on the knife's handle.

Another thing strikes me: it is obvious that Lucy regards herself as a woman who has nothing to lose. Her parents are dead, and she has admitted that she sees no future for her marriage. The relationship she might once have had with her brother has been pushed to breaking point by the events of the past couple of months, and as such she may consider herself in that most dangerous of positions: willing to do anything for what she believes to be right.

Does Lucy Spencer – Lucy Blackhurst – frighten me?

Of course she does. There is nothing more frightening than someone who has nothing left to lose; no one to be feared more greatly than a person who has nothing standing in their way.

'Is this one of your textbook analyses?' she asks, gesturing to the shelves of the bookcase.

'I've met plenty of narcissists in my time,' I tell her. 'They become easy to spot.'

'And my father demonstrated which of the relevant qualities, would you say?'

'Take your pick. He was self-interested, arrogant, manipulative. He lacked empathy and showed no remorse for any of his actions. He was capable of being charming, but only when it served the purpose of achieving his own aims.'

'Wow,' Lucy says, standing from the sofa to face me. 'You really are a walking textbook.'

'You're going to believe what you want anyway.'

'Give an example.'

'What?'

'An example of one of the above. Let's choose … arrogance, say.'

It is obvious to anyone that Lucy is an extremely troubled young woman, but I wonder just how deep these troubles run and what exactly she is capable of. Does her brother know how far she will go?

'You're asking me to recall something that happened twenty years ago?'

I wonder whether she's been drinking. Her movements are clumsy, her words at times erratic, and it wouldn't be the first time I've seen signs that she has a problem she isn't keen to acknowledge. Her mother drank: in her case, it was a form of escape. Christine mentioned her habit just the once, but when I tried to press the subject, she froze on me, regretting having spoken the words as soon as they left her mouth; just another of the truths she had tried to ignore.

'It shouldn't be too difficult, though, should it?' Lucy challenges. 'You seem to remember the details of my father's personality so well, you should be able to recall why you made the judgement that he was arrogant.'

In truth, I do remember all too well. I saw the extent of Stuart Blackhurst's dual personality one day at work, having just witnessed an exchange between him and one of my colleagues. He was nothing but politeness and charm in the small waiting room that sat between our offices, yet as soon as the door to mine was closed behind him, it was as though a switch had been flicked, and in place of the man who had moments earlier greeted my colleague with a wide smile and a door held open for her, there sat a man whose cold demeanour chilled the room by several degrees.

'I know what you are,' I said to him once, when Christine had left the two of us alone for a moment.

'And what's that exactly?'

'You're a bully. You might control Christine, but you won't control me.'

I remember him stepping nearer to me, so close that I could smell his aftershave. 'Is that so?' he said, leaning towards me, his face just inches from my own. 'And just what are you going to do about it?'

Stuart Blackhurst was the reason I left my office and my colleagues behind, and why I set up work from home, where Sean was more often than not close at hand. With him here, a few rooms away at most, I knew I was always safe.

An image enters my mind, unwanted: the hospital bed, the sheet, the teenage girl. When Lucy and James relived the allegation with me in this room, did they imagine the scenario in the way that I have, the way I have tried to erase from my consciousness for all these years? I still think about that girl, where she might be now – how Stuart Blackhurst might have affected the life she has gone on to lead.

I felt so sorry for her, as I felt so sorry for Lucy Green, the imagined daughter of 'Lydia'. And now that girl is standing here in front of me, her beliefs lined up before her like ammunition with which she is intent on destroying me, and though I realise how dangerous this woman might be, there is still a part of me that pities her.

'He spoke to me as though I was nothing,' I tell her. 'He thought he could intimidate me into silence, in the same way he had with your mother.'

This is all a waste of everyone's time, Karen – you realise that, don't you? She's never going anywhere. Where would she go?

Lucy laughs dismissively. 'Is that all you've got? Has it ever occurred to you that he might have spoken to you in that way because he could see what you were doing?'

'What was I doing?'

'Well, you and my mother were obviously working against him, whether you realised it at the time or not. She was using you as a witness, in a sense.'

'Witness to what?'

'This supposed abuse. Because no one else saw it, did they? Only you, because she wanted you to.'

'No one else saw it because your father was skilled at keeping it hidden. He wasn't the first.'

Lucy shakes her head, mirroring the motion by waving the knife slowly from side to side in front of her. 'There's something you don't seem to have considered – something that contradicts all your allegations. Why would he even come to you? The man you're describing would never agree to go to marriage guidance counselling. If he was as controlling as you claim he was, why would he have given my mother an opportunity to confide in you?'

Lucy looks triumphant, as though she has pulled out her trump card and brandished it in my face, leaving me with no defence in the argument. I wonder if this is the place from where all her belief in her father has stemmed: the fact that he came to marriage counselling, as though that alone is the mark of a good man and a loving husband.

'See?' she says, as petulant as a teenager and barely giving me time to answer her. 'It proves he loved her. It proves that everything else is bullshit. He came to you because he wanted to save his marriage. He wanted to help her, but she was already intent on destroying him. She wanted you to believe her bullshit – you were her only chance of getting away with murder.'

I hear her words, but it's James's face I focus on. It seems so obvious now what has been going on here, yet beneath their act as a married couple it was all concealed so cleverly. I remember the session during which the sexual assault allegation was raised, and how I waited in the corridor to listen to them talk.

Tell me that girl was lying.

I heard Lydia's insistence; her desperation to believe in her husband's innocence. Josh responded to her instruction with a wearied reluctance, as though this conversation was one that had been repeated so many times before.

How many times do I have to say it?

As many as it takes for me to believe you.

She wasn't a wife trying to believe in her husband's innocence: she was a daughter trying to convince her brother of their father's. The scale of the charade hits me in the gut, making me nauseous: the same roll of sickness that swept over me when the allegation was first mentioned. I had been there years earlier, listening to the same conversation. I had seen this before: confident, successful doctor, sexual assault allegation, abused wife. So why hadn't I seen what they were doing?

Never, not for a moment, did I believe the past would be capable of returning to me in this way. And yet perhaps I should have seen it. How many times had my mind drifted back to the days when I was in the presence of those people? Lucy looks like Christine, I can see that now – the narrow nose, the sharp features – and during our very first session together, didn't Josh look at me in a way that reminded me of Stuart Blackhurst, dragging me right back to that time and place, the expression on his face submerging me in memories? Something else occurs to me now. How many times did Josh criticise his wife's memory, suggesting that she didn't always remember things as they had happened? He knows. Though he may not have wanted to admit it before now, James knows what the truth is.

I see the doubt in his eyes, and everything continues to fall into place. All those times I thought of him as contradictory, never quite sure what to make of him. He was two people, Josh and James, and the two merged and blended, so that it was never clear even to him where one started and the other ended. When he spoke of Lydia's questionable memory, he was in a way confiding in me. He doesn't know what to believe; or he didn't then, at least. If there is anyone in this room who can help me now, it is James. He is my only hope.

'Your father was a narcissist,' I repeat, keeping my eyes fixed on Lucy's as I speak. 'A dangerous one at that. He came to my sessions because he saw no wrong in anything he had done – in fact, it was an opportunity for him to show off the control he'd developed over your mother down the years. He was proud of the suffering he was causing. He thought coming to me would teach your mother that there was nothing she could do to stop him. He was a sociopath, Lucy, despite everything people might have thought about him. He managed to fool his colleagues, his family … he even managed to fool the police. But I saw the real Stuart Blackhurst – I saw your father for everything he was. I know none of this is what you want to hear, but it's the truth.'

She steps closer, and I think for a moment that she might hit me. She doesn't. 'The man you're describing could never love his daughter the way my father loved me,' she says through clenched teeth. 'He loved me,' she repeats, tears spiking at the corners of her eyes, 'and you destroyed it. You destroyed everything.' Her face twists with a hatred that is venomous, her gaze boring into me. 'The truth is,' she says, spitting the words in my face, 'you saw what you wanted to see. You're the one with all the qualifications and the fancy letters after your name – surely you're not so stupid that you don't realise just how much your judgement of my father was influenced by what happened to you. Not every man is Damien Hunter, Karen.'

The words hit me, sending me reeling. Though I have spoken openly about my experiences within a controlling relationship, I have never revealed my ex-husband's name to anyone other than Sean. Damien Hunter has remained an anonymous character in the articles I have written, not deserving to be named or given attention.

I reach to the windowsill to steady myself while she stands there looking victorious, a violent pleasure being taken from my suffering. I feel exposed. Just how much does this woman know about my life?

'Drink your tea,' she says, waving the knife in front of me. 'Come on. A nice cup of tea makes everything better, doesn't it?'

'Whatever you believe,' I tell her, 'this has nothing to do with anything that might have happened to me. And you're wrong about your father – people are capable of all kinds of contradictions. Do you think someone who loves his mother isn't capable of killing a child? Or that someone who listens to classical music isn't capable of violence? You're a perfect example of how people can have two sides. You adored your father, anyone can see that, but you're still able to lie and cheat and deceive.' I watch as the smirk that has been fixed to her face slides away. 'You realise what you've done here, don't you? This whole charade, it makes a mockery of everyone who has suffered domestic abuse, men and women. Doing that to yourself,' I say, gesturing to her stomach. 'It's sick.'

She leans over me, the knife just inches from my face. 'Drink your tea, Karen.'

She stands back and waits for me to pick up the cup. I glance at James, willing him to stop this madness. The fact is that no matter how crazy this woman might be, there is truth in some of what she says. I saw a narcissist in the character James played because that's what I am trained to see. I mistook his confusion and his vulnerability – his anger with his sister and her manipulation of the situation – for violence and control. I was wrong. I admit that I was wrong.

But where their father was concerned, I know I made no mistake. Stuart Blackhurst was the most skilled sociopath I have ever had the misfortune to encounter. He knew that I saw through him – that I was the only person to see past the persona he had so skilfully created for himself – and on several occasions he made attempts to bully me into silence. I continued my work with the couple because I saw the situation that Christine was trapped in. I told her to leave her husband when I saw the danger she was in, and the possible future trouble that lay ahead of her. I was trying to help her, though I failed in my efforts. I have known for all these years that I failed her, carrying that weight with me like a lead lung. I failed her children, I realised that too.

And now they are here with me – they have been here with me for months – and I realise that nothing I can say or do will undo the years of suffering they have endured.

'Your tea,' Lucy says, jabbing the knife in my direction.

I take another sip, and then another when she makes it clear that she is in control here. I am a puppet, just like James, each movement carried out at her say-so.

'Now say you got it wrong.'

He was a good man.

My mind flits back to that initial meeting with them all those months ago, and to that first strained conversation in which so much hostility was emptied into this room. Once again it seems so obvious what was going on, yet their performance was so convincing that I was unable to see through it. *He was a good man*, she said, and I sat there believing that she was referring to Josh: to the husband who was sitting opposite her, being spoken about in the past tense as though the person he had once been no longer existed. Yet all the time she was talking about Stuart Blackhurst. She was trying to convince her brother that their father had been a good man, and if he needed convincing of the fact, it is further evidence that James's opinion is not fixed even after all these years.

I recall what she said about James when she was describing their 'son'.

Beneath it all he's just a scared little boy desperate for his daddy's love.

And now his reaction to those words makes sense. She was describing him: the boy he was and the man he has become. She was mocking him, goading him; belittling him in order to shape him into the person she needed him to be: the person who would come here with her to perform this charade, all with the aim of seeking some perverse sense of revenge. And to begin with he played along with her game. He wore the right clothes, he said the right things; he occasionally slipped up, but I was too naïve to see it for what it was.

Just how controlled has he been by his sister over the years? She made a comment about sacrifice, about sticking by him through everything. I know enough of the care system to know that it fails too many children, and I wonder now whether Lucy played on his vulnerability and the threat of separation that must have hung over them. Was she the only person he felt able to rely on after his parents' death? She was his sole source of stability and continuity: it seems reasonable to assume he would depend on her for security. He has been failed multiple times, and one of those times was by me.

But one thing I am sure of, now more than ever: James is not convinced of his father's innocence. He never has been. And where his sister holds a hatred for me that is keenly embedded within her heart, I am unconvinced her brother feels the same.

'This has gone too far,' I tell him.

'Say it!' Lucy yells at me like a madwoman, her cheeks burning scarlet. Her brother flinches at the noise of her rage.

'I got it wrong,' I say. She steps back and away from me, smiling as though once again she has gained some sort of victory. She is right that I got things wrong, but not in the way she believes. I thought that Josh – James – was the dangerous one, but I was so far from the truth of it, and that has been my biggest mistake.

'Do you feel guilty yet, Karen? Two people died because of you, all because you were too blind to see what was staring you in the face. You believed me, didn't you? The abuse, the bruises, the fear. All of it. If I was able to convince you of my suffering so easily, surely you can see now that she lied to you as well? What did she tell you about him?'

'I saw the bruises for myself, Lucy. I saw what he had done to her.'

'You saw my bruises as well. What you choose to see and what is actually real aren't always the same thing, are they? Everything she said to you was designed to manipulate you. The victim act, the lies, the tears. All of it was a performance.'

I am shaking my head. Her words are those of a fantasist; someone who has been so blindsided by her father's charm that she is unable to see even the faintest glimpse of the person he really was. 'To what end?' I challenge.

'Killing him. It was no act of defence, was it? She'd planned it. The marriage counselling, it was all in preparation for the final act of getting rid of him. She thought you'd be able to get her out of trouble – that with your glowing character reference and an account of my father's so-called abuse, she could get away with murder.'

I am shaking my head, my eyes still pleading with James to try to gain some control over his sister. Yet I realise he can't. Even if the knife wasn't still gripped in her fist, he seems powerless where she is concerned. Whatever she might be, Lucy is the only person he has left in this world.

'So why did she kill herself, Lucy? If all she had wanted was your father dead, why take her own life like she did?'

I can remember as vividly as though it was this morning that day I opened the newspaper and read of Stuart Blackhurst's death, and though my heart held a breath before my brain absorbed the details, I already knew the circumstances that had led up to the event. Christine had told me the last time I had seen her that she was going to do it: she was going to apply for the divorce papers. I can still recall now the sense of euphoria I felt in my chest for this woman who had been so controlled and demoralised by the person she'd believed had loved her more than anyone else. The words I had spoken to her – the reality I had repeated until she could no longer ignore it – were finally being acknowledged.

You can't stay with a violent man for the sake of your children. You may think that by holding the family together you are doing the right thing, but what are you teaching them about marriage if they see you stay with a man who treats you so badly and makes you feel the way your husband clearly does? Show your children courage and strength. Show them you are worth more than this. They may not thank you for it now, but they will realise in time that leaving him was as much for their sakes as it was for your own.

She was going to escape him, and I was the person who was setting her free. I would save her. I would save her children, in a way I wasn't able to save my own child.

A month later, he was dead. Six weeks after that, so was she. She took a lethal cocktail of tablets that she emptied from various bottles in the bathroom cupboard, and was found lying on her son's bed, a photograph of her children on the duvet by her open hand.

Before Christine Blackhurst took her own life, the police came to talk to me, as they did with so many of the people who had been known to the couple. I told them the truth as I had seen it: that Stuart Blackhurst was manipulative and controlling and that his wife had endured years of emotional, psychological and physical abuse that had been kept concealed from the outside world, in part by the skilled performance he played and in part by Christine's all-consuming sense of shame. It didn't seem to matter to the police: I was one voice in contradiction of a hundred glowing character references. Stuart Blackhurst was a charming man, admired by his neighbours and respected by his colleagues. A false allegation of sexual abuse had been made against him: the girl had admitted she'd lied. Poor man, an allegation like that could stick, even when proved false, but he was supported at work – pitied, even – and everyone rallied around to ensure that his reputation remained intact.

There was no evidence of abuse against his wife – no reports made to the police, no photographic evidence of any physical injuries inflicted upon her. It was her word against his reputation, and what was she? Just a housewife and a mother; just a strange, slightly off-beat woman who had shut herself away from the world some time earlier. I owed her everything. Christine Blackhurst was me: she was what my life might have become.

Despite my best efforts to convince the police that it was manslaughter, Christine was charged with murder. She was released on bail and permitted to return home under a set of rules that restricted her from certain freedoms, one of which included seeing her children. I went to the house to speak to her, and remember being struck by how normal the place was, with no evidence of any of the horrors that had taken place inside those four walls. Her children had been taken into care pending the result of her trial.

She let me into the house, but only to hide from the neighbours the scene that would unfold. I see her now as vividly as I saw her that day in the hallway: still in her nightdress, her eyes dark and sunken, red-rimmed with tears. She had always been a slight woman, but further weight loss had left her frail and appearing a decade older than her years. She looked at me in a way that no one ever had before or ever has since, with an expression of such pained contempt, as though I was the root of all her life's tragedy; which in a way I was.

They're going to find me guilty. My children will be without a mother.

I told her what I had been trying to do, that I had stressed to the authorities what had been happening inside this house. I explained how I might help her during her trial, but she already knew that nothing had been documented. Counselling involves the safety of privacy, and what I hear is spoken for my ears only. I keep no records, though it is standard practice for some, I believe that doing so goes against everything the very nature of my profession represents. Kept in my head, the details of other people's lives are safe from prying eyes and ears. My methods have been designed to protect, yet they have had the opposite effect. Where Christine and Stuart Blackhurst were concerned, I had no proof of anything. Without evidence, my statements meant nothing.

You said everything was going to be okay. You told me I was doing the right thing.

Christine sobbed through her sentences, each word barely audible as it fell into the next. I remember trying to reach for an arm to steady her, and how she swiped my hand away from hers, her nails catching the back of it and breaking the skin, two small spots of blood bubbling to the surface. It felt like the least I deserved. And I remember what I noticed then for the first time, fixed to the wall that ran up the stairs: two photographs framed in gold, one of a boy, and the other of a girl.

She had never told me what her children were called, and her husband had never named them either. Even within the confines of the four walls of my office, everything she had done was with the aim of keeping them safe. And with five little words I had managed to shatter everything she had strived so hard for.

You need to leave him.

I recall the last words she ever said to me.

I should never have listened to you.

I failed Christine's children once, but I can't let that happen again. They deserve to know the truth, regardless of whether it is what they want to hear.

As though stealing a thought from my brain, James speaks for the first time in ages. 'He did it, didn't he?' he says, ignoring the look his words receive from Lucy. 'All of it. The sexual assault allegation as well?'

I nod. 'I'm sorry, James, I really am. But I think you already knew.'

He nods and turns to his sister, who is crying now; angry, silent tears rolling down her made-up face. Memories of their third session come rushing back. It was Lucy who brought up the subject of the allegation, but it was James who responded to it with such anger and resentment. I assumed he was adamant about maintaining his innocence, yet I see it so differently now. He wasn't angry with the girl; he was angry with his father. He was angry at Lucy for trying to dissuade him from a truth he knew to be real.

'She admitted she'd lied,' Lucy says.

When they relived their parents' marriage in my house – when they moved through the motions of replaying their memories, each in their own way trying to persuade the other that their version of events was the correct one – they changed the details of the past, enough for me to fail to see what was happening right in front of me.

'Did she, though?' I challenge her. 'Did she really admit that, or did she say it because she feared that no one would believe her or that she might end up worse off if she tried to pursue justice? Things were very different back then. She wasn't allowed anonymity in the way she would be now.' I turn my attention to James, knowing that if either of them is to believe what I am saying, it will be him. 'I have no proof of this, but I think your father might have paid her off to keep her quiet. He could afford it, and your mother would never have noticed – she had no access to their finances.'

'*His* finances.'

I ignore Lucy as I continue to appeal to whatever element of reason her brother might possess. 'It was the nineties; things were very different back then. You've seen how many men have got away with this sort of crime over the years – it's been all over the news. How many so-called celebrities have we seen having to face up to their crimes decades later, people who no one would have suspected because they were so popular and well respected? Things have changed. If your father was still alive now, perhaps he'd finally be made culpable too.'

'Don't you dare say another word!' Lucy rushes towards me like a charging animal. She raises the knife, but it is knocked from her hand by James, who lunges towards her with an extended arm, swiping the blade from her grasp. It hits the carpet as he flails back, blood dripping from the cut that has been sliced across his palm.

'Everything she's saying is right,' he gasps, clenching his hand into a fist to try to staunch the flow.

'You're pathetic,' she snaps, spitting the words at him. She drags her sleeve across her face and steps back, trying to regain her composure. 'We all know about your sad little schoolboy crush. Has she got you so excited you're willing to forget what she did?'

She moves to retrieve the fallen knife.

'But what did she do, Lucy, really? She was trying to help.'

'By splitting our family up?'

'By trying to protect us.'

Lucy laughs snidely and throws her hands in the air in an exaggerated, false gesture of acceptance. 'Oh, okay, that's all right then. Thank you,' she says, turning to me. 'Thank you for helping protect me from a man who did nothing but love me. Thank you for killing both my parents and leaving us in a series of shitty care homes that did nothing but fuck us both up. Have you forgotten what happened to you?' she shouts, turning her attention back to her brother. 'Have you forgotten all the shit you had to put up with in those places?' She steps towards him, reaches out a hand and presses her fingertips to his nose. He flinches at the touch of her skin upon his and backs away from her.

'They broke his nose,' she says, turning to me. 'Some of the other kids, they were trying to hold his head down one of the toilets. For a skinny little thing he was pretty strong – he kept trying to fight them off. It would have been a lot less painful just to let them have their few minutes of fun.' She turns back to her brother. 'And who was there for you, James? Who was the only person to ever look out for you? It wasn't her protecting you then, was it?'

James glances at the knife back in Lucy's hands, wary of the way it is being waved around with the careless abandon of a child in possession of a lit sparkler. The pain on his face says he is aware now just how deeply a surface wound can sting. He won't push her any more, not when he knows she is still capable of worse.

'I know what you did for me, and I'm grateful for it,' he says. 'But I never realised I'd be in so much debt for it.'

She opens her mouth, her eyes narrowed with indignation. 'I could have left you. They wanted to split us up plenty of times, but I made sure it never happened.'

'Perhaps it would have been better if you had.'

The look on her face changes in an instant, her anger crushed beneath a weight of hurt.

'All you've done is try to control me. That's not love, Lucy. That's what Dad did to Mum.' He looks at me, searching for an answer to a question he hasn't asked. I nod. I don't need to say anything; they both know the truth. It occurs to me that these two adults are still children, repressed by a childhood that left them with permanent scars. The ways in which they've dealt with the aftermath of everything they were exposed to have obviously been very different.

I move tentatively from the side of the room, confident that for the moment at least, Lucy won't try anything stupid. I pull a handful of tissues from the box on the sideboard and pass them to James, who bunches them in his hand and presses them to his palm. They quickly turn red; the wound is deeper than I realised. Giving up on the bloodied tissues, he shoves them into the pocket of his trousers and holds out his uninjured hand to his sister.

'No one else needs to get hurt,' he says.

She looks at his outstretched arm before turning the knife and placing the handle in his palm. Then, leaning to the table in front of me, she pushes my teacup towards me. There is only a small amount left in it, and she swirls it around for a moment before putting it back down.

'Too late for that,' she says, looking at me blankly. 'You may as well finish your tea, Karen. Enjoy it ... it's your last.'

She steps wordlessly past her brother and leaves the room. The two of us wait, stunned into a moment's silence, before my attention is drawn back to the teacup and to the possibility of what has been implied. We hear the front door slam behind Lucy as she leaves the house; I wait a beat, anticipating her return, but she is gone.

'You should have told me who you were. All this could have been avoided.'

He says nothing. We both know what I've said is untrue: Lucy would have kept going, with or without him.

'What does Lucy's husband do?' I ask quietly, though I already know the answer to the question. I need to hear it again, to have my suspicions confirmed as more than simply paranoia.

'He works in pharmaceuticals.' James is also looking at the table, his face telling me he is thinking the same as I am. He stares at the teacup, his words – Lucy's words – assuming a greater possibility.

My stomach makes a strange and alien noise and I feel something like a cramp grip my insides, making me nauseous. I look at the dregs of the tea on the table in front of me; they stare accusingly back, taunting me with their silence. Has she done what we suspect she has? Have I been poisoned? I made the tea; Lucy didn't go anywhere near it, other than to carry the tray into this room. Surely in that time she wasn't able to do anything to it, though I realise there have been plenty of times my eyes have failed to see what has been right in front of me. If Lucy is capable of the level of deceit that has been played out in this room during the past few months, it seems likely she is more than able to perform a sleight of hand that has gone unnoticed.

'I don't feel well.'

I try to shake myself from the thought of what might have been done. She left the insinuation in the air, made more of a threat by the words she didn't speak. But Lucy tells lies, doesn't she? She has been lying to me for months. She has been lying to herself for years.

She's going to lie to you.

'James, please. I need your help.'

I continue to stare at the almost empty teacup on the table, as though I will find an answer in the remnants of the drink. Nausea turns in my stomach and a dull pulse builds in my brain as James takes his mobile phone from his pocket and dials 999. I hear him ask for an ambulance, though the words are muffled as though I am hearing them from under water. I feel as if I am somewhere else, another day, another life; no longer really me, as if all this is happening to someone else.

'Okay,' I hear James say to whoever has answered his call. 'I'll tell her. Karen,' he says, turning to me, his voice laced with panic. 'You need to make yourself sick. Now.'

I leave the room without speaking to him and go to the downstairs toilet, where I stick my fingers down my throat. I didn't eat breakfast this morning, and my empty stomach burns as I retch. Bile escapes me, but there is little more.

'Karen.'

James is in the hallway.

'I am so sorry,' he says through the closed door. 'This wasn't what I wanted. I wanted the truth. I wanted to know where I come from.'

I stand, flush the toilet and wash my hands. Pressing my palms to the edge of the sink, I lean forward and study my eyes in the mirror, as though I might be able to detect signs of poisoning. I realise it is futile; I have no idea what I am looking for. Yet as I gaze at myself, I see something that has been hidden for the three years since Sean has been gone. Behind the tiredness that waters my eyes and the sadness that sits upon my features, there is life. Maybe I hadn't realised it until now, but more than ever, I want to live.

When I open the door, James is there waiting for me, and for the first time ever I find myself able to believe his words without questioning them first. Whatever he is guilty of, I accept that he had no intention of things going this far.

'You already knew the truth,' I say.

His eyes are cast downwards, knowing that what I say is right. I wonder what he has apologised for. Is it these last few months of lies, or is it this, now: the possibility of what his sister has done, of what she is capable of?

I go to the kitchen and he follows. I open the fridge and pour myself a glass of milk, standing at the sink and sipping it carefully, trying not to linger on the thought of what Lucy might have laced my tea with. I think I remember reading once that milk can help dilute detergents that have been ingested, though I have no idea whether this is simply an old wives' tale.

'They said they won't be long,' James tell me, as though my fear has been uttered and has broken the silence that sits between us.

'*The Playing Field*,' I say, thinking aloud.

'Sorry?'

'*The Playing Field*,' I repeat, my stomach turning with something that feels like more than fear alone. 'You remembered the name of the play your father took your mother to see.'

It wasn't easy to do, but once I learned the couple's true identities, I managed to trace the play and the theatre at which it was shown. It ran there for five nights during May of 1985; it took eight phone calls and three former members of staff to help me find a record of it. It might seem trivial, but it mattered. It matters. It means that at some point James was told about it, presumably by his mother, and that decades later, he still remembers.

It means his memory is reliable; far more so, apparently, than his sister's. Where doubts have begun to creep into my consciousness, certainty steps in to smother it. I made no mistake about Stuart Blackhurst, though I have made many about his son.

'There are plenty of things I remember.'

I recall the way he raised the subject of the play; the way he challenged Lucy to remember what it was called. He was questioning her memory, her reliability, suggesting even then that she wasn't to be trusted.

'You were trying to tell me something, weren't you? Even back then at that first meeting.'

'I know what Lucy is,' he tells me, 'but I wanted to believe her. I've always wanted to believe her. She's all I've got left. And no one wants to think their parent is capable of the kind of sins my father was guilty of, do they? You can pretend it isn't real for a while, but you can't avoid the truth for ever. I've lived in the shadow of what he was my whole life. I can't do it any more.'

I lean against the worktop and close my eyes at the sound of Sean's voice in my head. We sat in this kitchen together three weeks before he died, drinking lager he'd been told he shouldn't drink while having the conversation both of us had wanted to put off for as long as possible.

You've got to live your life, Karen. You have so many years left ahead of you. Make them good ones.

Every word he spoke sounded wrong to my ears. How could I even contemplate carrying on after he was gone? When his life ended, so would mine. In all my adult years, the only happiness I had known had come after I had met him; I didn't know how to exist in a world where he wasn't. A future without him was a future I didn't want to face.

I found ways to fill my days, and a purpose in helping the couples I would invite into my home, but in the three years that have passed since that conversation in this room, I realise I haven't done what Sean requested of me. I have existed, moving through the motions of everyday life in a pretence at living. And only now, with the past standing in front of me, do I understand that he was right.

'You're not your father, James.'

The tension eases from his face; he looks relieved, grateful even. With just those few words I seem to remove a doubt that has been hanging over him, possibly since he was just a child. The violence he has almost been capable of, the anger he carries with him, never appearing to know where might be safe to leave it, the uncertainty of his childhood that has shaped the adult he has become – all these things he has kept with him, gripping on to them for fear that losing them might leave him adrift; hating their closeness for the possibility that they make him a product of where he has come from.

Where James – where Josh – was once so confusing in all his contradictions, now it seems he couldn't be easier for me to read. He hasn't wanted to admit to himself what his father was for fear that he is something like him, that there may be a part of him that is a reincarnation of Stuart Blackhurst, a man he has tried to emulate during these past couple of months, having spent a lifetime attempting to hide from the truth of what he was.

'He had a chance to put things right. He never took it. You need to live your life now.'

The irony of my words is interrupted by knocking at the front door, and as James goes to let the paramedics into the house, I know I won't let Lucy Blackhurst do this to me. Her family has marred so much of my past; they don't get to take my future. This isn't how it ends.

A LETTER FROM VICTORIA

Dear Reader,

I want to say a huge thank you for choosing to read *The Divorce*. If you enjoyed it, and want to keep up to date with all my latest releases, just sign up at the following link. Your email address will never be shared and you can unsubscribe at any time.

www.bookouture.com/victoria-jenkins

Writing *The Divorce* has been a new challenge for me, having moved from police procedurals to give a psychological thriller a try. I love reading this kind of book, so it seemed a natural progression for me to have a go at writing one. With so few characters in the story, I was able to get right into the mind of each, and I have enjoyed developing their stories and their secrets.

Research for the book involved reading about cases of coercive control within marriages, something that wasn't considered a criminal offence until just a few years ago. The real-life stories I read were harrowing and heartbreaking, with victims of domestic violence and emotional abuse in some cases enduring decades of horrendous treatment that went unnoticed by family and friends and ignored by authorities. It is easy for someone who has never been a victim of domestic abuse to ask, 'Why didn't she/he just leave?' but the issues are sadly far more complex than that.

I hope you loved *The Divorce*; if you did, I would be very grateful if you could write a review. I'd love to hear what you think, and it makes such a difference helping new readers to discover one of my books for the first time.

I love hearing from my readers – you can get in touch on my Facebook page, through Twitter, Goodreads or my website.

Thanks,
Victoria Jenkins

 victoriajenkinswriter

@vicwritescrime

ACKNOWLEDGEMENTS

Firstly, a massive thank you to my editor, Jenny Geras, for suggesting I give a psychological thriller a go and for supporting me so fully through every stage of this process. This book has felt like a real team effort, and I have loved writing it. Thanks also to my agent, Anne, who is always there for me in moments of panic (which are regular!). To my fellow Bookouture authors, thank you for all your ongoing support (did I mention moments of panic?) and for never failing to make me laugh – in particular, thanks to Shalini Boland and Angie Marsons for offering advice and guidance when it has been much needed. To Kim Nash and Noelle Holten, thanks for looking out for me on both a professional and personal level – the Bookouture family really is a special one.

Thanks to Liz Hunt for sharing her knowledge and expertise in marriage counselling; your insight was invaluable to the writing of this book. Thanks also to my first ever beta reader, the lovely Jo Quinn – expect another in a few months' time!

To my own family, a huge thank you as always for the babysitting that allows me to get these books written – I couldn't do it without you. Steve, you are a brilliant father and the best husband; you have always encouraged me to follow my dreams, and without you none of this would be possible. Thank you.

Dad, you will always be with me in everything I write and everything I do. I miss you every day, but I like to think you're up there somewhere watching Mia grow. I hope we make you proud.

Life has continued to deal blows this year, with the loss of my neighbour and friend, Joy. I miss your smile and hearing your voice at the end of the phone. This one, lovely lady, is for you.

Made in the USA
Columbia, SC
27 March 2021

35152999R00126